I0525575

# Until Death Do Us Apart

## By
## Cade North

STORY MERCHANT BOOKS
LOS ANGELES
2019

STORY MERCHANT BOOKS

Author Contact Information:
Cade North
cade@cadenorth.com

Copyright © 2019 by Cade North
All rights reserved.

No part of this book may be reproduced or transmitted in any form or by any means, electronic or mechanical, including photocopying, recording, or by any information storage and retrieval system, without the express written permission of the author.

ISBN: 978-1-970157-02-4

Story Merchant Books
400 S. Burnside Avenue #11B
Los Angeles, CA 90036

http://www.storymerchantbooks.com

Interior formatting by IndieDesignz.com

# Dedication

First this work is dedicated to my two remarkable children who are growing into even more amazing adults. As ever you are my greatest inspiration as well as my favorite distraction. Always trust your own integrity and resilience to take you wherever your hearts lead you.

I also dedicate this book to Sherene Singh Mitchell, who—without fail— has splashed through life's puddles with me since the 1990s. Come what may; we will get through it together, my friend.

# Acknowledgements

Endless thanks and love go out to my real-life go-to team: Sherene Singh Mitchell, Amy Fiorani Galvan, Gail Hug, and Jean Benacker. Not only are these people some of the brightest and most talented people I know but, even more importantly, they always had my back over the course of many, many years. As ever, my strength reflects my support.

Much appreciation also goes out to John and Kate Campbell who read then gave feedback on numerous drafts of this manuscript.

Further thanks and love go out to my real-life best gays—Morris Hylton and Mike Hastings. Very few people are as authentic and entertaining as the two of you. Our hilarious conversations served as a rich source of inspiration while writing much of this book's dialogue.

By no means should I forget to mention Rob Johnson, my formal personal trainer. Not only did he help whip my super-sized butt into its younger shape but, in the process, he became a fun and insightful friend. Though we live far apart now, my wish for you, Rob, is that your life is never as hard as your abs!

Lastly, love and light go out from Bonecrusher to the other Bos from our DePauw days. These Bos—Carrie Schaefer Bucki, Renee Schuler, and Kristina Uland—inspired and participated in my earliest attempts at fictionalizing real life. May we have more Mu Iota adventures in the future, my friends!

# Table of Contents

Always treat people with integrity and thoughtful consideration. First off, I'm pretty sure that's what Jesus, the 7-11 Night Manager, would do (although, to be fair, 7-11 Jesus says Bible Jesus also subscribes to the same notion). Plus, sometimes Karma has a Ph.D. which means there's a pretty good chance that brainy bitch is going to write a book.

Sloane Noah

# The Celibate Seductress

## Prologue

As far back as I could remember, my life story never unfolded like everyone else's. Instead, my life was like a Lifetime movie mistakenly played by the cast of Saturday Night Live—still packed with unlikely drama but absurd to the point of ridiculousness. Since my history was consistent only in its convoluted nature, I guess I shouldn't have been surprised when I found myself in my late 20s, married, so randy I felt like I needed to wear a warning label as a service to society, and, well, celibate.

Despite "Men Always Want Sex" being the official headline when it comes to sexuality and the sexes, it isn't true. While that's how the story is commonly told, there are men who are not even remotely interested in sex. Did you know that was a thing? Until I was married, I didn't. As I made that discovery, I also learned that when you've committed to forever with someone who doesn't mesh with you on some basic level—such as agreeing on what constitutes an adequate sex life—then forever becomes far longer than you ever imagined.

Still, since we already had 2 children together, this mismatched partnership wasn't one I was willing to let go of easily. As it turned out, the happiness of these two cherub-faced people we made was more important to me than my own. So, 9 years into the marriage, I was still locked in a relentless optimism set towards making the marriage work.

That meant I was still struggling to lure my husband into bed more often than the inescapable once-a-year routine. I had my theories as to why traditional seduction—cleavage-bearing lingerie or shaving into a landing strip down south—didn't work with the man I was legally bound to in sickness and in health. Regardless, the fact was I desperately wanted something—anything - to work because I was in a silent race, trying to outrun the hopelessness I could feel closing in on me.

One day, I decided to test out a new theory. I hypothesized effective seduction may require the proper setting. Therefore, if the bedroom was an enticing place then I reasoned that perhaps I may be successful in enticing my husband into a horizontal and naked position. To that end, I'd exchanged our bed's worn, flannel sheets and our hand-me-down quilt for an absurdly expensive 800 count silk sheets topped with a silk, down-filled comforter. After slipping the last sinuous, silk pillow sham onto its pillow, I stood back, surveying my work. Satisfyingly, it now looked like a high-class den of iniquity rather than a place of simple function.

Shortly after tucking my twin 2-year-olds into bed that evening, I slithered into a black, stringy number that was substantially less comfortable but vastly sluttier than my other eveningwear, lit and arranged some scented candles on the nightstand, then said a quick prayer to the Universe that this attempt might work.

In the dancing glow of the candlelight, I stared into the tall, wood-framed mirror standing like a sentinel in the corner of our room. Turning slowly to one side and then to the other, I tried to see myself from a man's perspective. At 29 years old, my runner's legs were tight and fit but not overly muscular. My toes were pedicured, my lips glossed. Even though "my assets" still pointed up, I suspected gravity would change that in about a decade, so I knew I needed to make these perky years count. *This is as good as I get*, I thought.

I chose the perfume my husband, Tom, bought for me for Christmas, sprayed it into the air then stepped through the scented mist. Spritzing into the air again, I repeated the ritual. Properly fragranced, polished, glossed, as well as strapped complexly into lingerie I was fairly certain must be designed by NASA, I took a deep breath before starting down the stairs.

Walking up behind Tom, who was working on our desktop computer, I pressed my chest against his upper back as I slid my open hands down his chest. He was a tall, athletic man. So tall, in fact, when sitting his head was almost at the same level as mine when standing. Slowly but lightly, I kissed the back of his neck.

I said nothing but made a small, "Mmm…" sound.

"What's up?' he asked, not looking away from the computer monitor.

"Well, I was just wondering if *you* might be ready for *bed*?" I asked, nipping his ear with my teeth.

After a brief pause, "Nah, I'll be up in a bit."

"But you haven't seen the new bedding yet," I pushed.

"I'm sure I'll love it," he said, kissing my cheek dismissively while his eyes held firm to the monitor.

*Only the weak surrender*, I thought.

"What do you think of my new pjs?" I asked, stepping back and slowly turning in a circle. He pulled his eyes away from the computer and glanced at me.

"Very stringy. Did you borrow a shrimp fisherman's nets?" Tom asked, turning back to the computer.

"Well, I'm fairly certain those fishermen have never pulled in a catch like me," I said flirtatiously.

"You are a catch," he said, patting me dismissively on the bum. "I'll be up in a bit."

Even after 7 years, this rejection ritual still stung. Walking back toward the stairs, I repeated silently to myself, "It's about him, not about me. It's about him, not about me," and hoped with an expanding desperation that what I said was true.

Back in our empty room, I slipped between the fine, new sheets. The cool taupe silk snaked across my skin. Embraced in luxury I'd never enjoyed before, I sunk into my pillow and watched the shadows from the candlelight quivering on the wall. *I do feel pretty in this big, beautiful bed. Pretty, pretty, and alone. Why is marriage so lonely?* I skimmed my fingertips along the comforter's fluid surface. *Wasn't silk supposed to be erotic? Or at least as erotic as fabrics go. And it's a natural product; good for the environment. So, I may be an embarrassingly failed seductress but at least I'm a good steward for the environment,* I thought.

"Yeah, because environmentally-friendly bedding will keep me warm at night," I said to the empty room as I floated my hands back across the comforter. Then I laughed aloud at the bad joke because, environmentally-friendly or not, bedding *would* keep me warm at night. *Even when wearing what apparently looks like a fisherman's nets, I'll be snug and comfortable. Yep, all snug while slowly getting old, saggy, and, eventually, having my vagina boarded up like some dilapidated, abandoned house.*

Beyond its sensual reputation, there was something I didn't know about silk fabric. As my doctor later explained, "In its processing, silk is often treated with formaldehyde. That's because, formaldehyde resins introduce unique qualities to fabrics such as being anti-static, anti-wrinkle, and perspiration-resistance."

In addition to the benefits of treating fabric with harsh chemicals, the other thing I didn't know was that the Universe was rolling up her sleeves as she chose me to be one of those who would experience formaldehyde's substantial downside.

In the dark, I woke suddenly. Not knowing what awakened me, I listened to the night. It was quiet except for my husband lightly snoring from the far side of our king-sized bed. Just then, I gasped, and my breath caught in my chest. I tried to take another breath, but that caught too. Every time I took a breath, it was as though the air could not reach my lungs. Panic ignited in my rapidly constricting chest.

*What was going on? Was I having an anxiety attack? Or maybe a heart attack?* I gasped again and, alarm choking me, I started to cry. Since I didn't have enough air in my lungs for a healthy, chest-heaving cry, tears streamed from my eyes, but my lungs remained dedicated to trying to claim any bit of oxygen from the air they could. I leaned up on my elbows before sitting up fully. Leaning on one arm, with my other hand resting on top of the crushing pain in my chest, I fought for air.

My stirring and wheezing woke Tom.

"What are you doing? You woke me up," he said accusingly.

"I'm having trouble breathing," I said in a panicked rush.

No answer.

"Maybe I'm having an anxiety attack or something," I suggested between gasps.

He rolled over roughly, smashing his pillow into a more pleasing configuration.

"Well, you are keeping me awake."

"I can't breathe right," I gasped.

Another pause.

"You know how to breathe; just do it!" Tom barked.

It was then I got up from our shared bed for the last time. In confused anger and panic, I rushed into the vacant guest room. Sitting on the empty bed's edge, I closed my eyes and concentrated on breathing slowly, deliberately. Since I was still conscious, I could only assume my lungs were getting *some* air. This thought was oddly comforting because on a scale ranging from alive to dead, my needle hadn't hit the bottom just yet. On I went, breathing in slowly, willing air into my lungs, then exhaling with the wish that the next breath would come more easily. My burdened chest and lungs ached. *I have to breathe*, I thought. *I'm not going to die like this—as the world's most inappropriately dressed nun.* So, I stubbornly raked in air as best I could and rasped it back out.

After a time, my breathing became less strained and the vice on my chest loosened. Eventually, with my breaths almost normal and exhausted from the struggle for oxygen, I crawled under the comforter on the guest bed. As I faded into a weary sleep, I thought vaguely of my husband. *In truth, did he not care if I was having trouble breathing?* Although I never actively considered it before, having an interest in preventing my untimely death now seemed like a desirable quality to look for in a partner. I could envision my future dating website ad: "Brainy chick looking for someone I can depend upon to call 9-1-1 as needed."

# Beacon for the Absurd
## Chapter 1

've always wanted a boring life. Seriously. Every year, I work to make life more predictable. My ultimate goal was to create such an easy-to-anticipate and smooth existence that cause and effect are tightly and clearly linked. In my personal utopia, raises or promotions consistently follow hard work. Similarly, kindness towards others guarantees kindness in return.

Despite my desire for the mundane and expected, my life never played this out. Instead, I was a lightning rod for the shocking and comically bizarre. Even my strengths and talents were laced with ironic and shifting counterweights, keeping me off balance. For instance, I was brainy enough to become a college professor. In the predictable world I dreamt of, that meant my future would undoubtedly include a steady rhythm of teaching, research, and publishing study findings until I earned my way to a boring retirement. Despite having the capability as well as the will, the counterbalance was my erratic yet largely looming case of Attention Deficit Disorder (A.D.D.).

A.D.D. must be unionized because it doesn't work seven days a week. On its days off, I interpret data and write precise articles making innovative connections and new insights. When A.D.D. is on the clock, though, suddenly I'm an Alzheimer's-prone squirrel monkey, racing around in a confused panic. As soon as I turn my attention toward one task, I can't remember, even vaguely, what I am supposed to do. Staring blankly at said task, eventually so much time passes I must accept my mind cannot or will not access whatever internal database is going to give me the information needed to actually do it, even if I've done that very thing successfully one thousand times before.

Then ineptitude-based anxiety hits, spurring me to the next task. Even if that second task is as profoundly simple as reading email, my mind derails and goes all static-y. Upon opening a message, I do not see an organized series of sentences. Instead, it's as though the words have all been heaped into a pile. While I can sift through and read each individual word I pick up, this mound of words does not produce any coherent meaning. Even if I could follow the strings of words as they were written, my A.D.D. memory will not hold more than two words at a time, erasing the first part of the sentence's meaning by the time I've reached the sentence's end. Then if the message asks me to do some specific thing, for some reason the A.D.D. fog makes the idea that someone is expecting me to do some task—which at this moment I am incapable of doing— overwhelming for me. As my anxious and exhausted state expands then heightens, my body needs a reboot, a complete shut-down. The only possible rescue from the impending despair or anxiety attack is the act of taking a simple nap. If, and only if, I can press this restart button, can I then try again at the possibility of normal functioning.

These inconvenient facts about the way my brain runs are obviously at complete odds with the expectations of the modern work world. My body was not wired to operate well under the strict workplace norms requiring responsibilities to be efficiently completed between 8 A.M. and 5 P.M., with the neatly-scheduled noon hour for an employee's mind to wander. A.D.D., a super villain, my own personal Lex Luthor living in my head, wants no part of that tradition. Regardless of the circumstances, this villain will not bend to my will. In part, this is why I became a professor.

Since academics tend to keep odd hours, this helps me work around my brain's shortcomings. Also, professors, in my experience, are a lot like overbred dogs. They tend to have a lot of odd quirks not present in the general population. Apparently, these quirky characteristics are the trade-off for having one thing you do really well. For instance, one of my friends is a young but brilliant statistician. When it comes to statistical analysis, his abilities are unbounded. Despite his giftedness with numbers, his brilliant mind cannot tell time on a regular, analog clock. While droves of second graders across the country master this skill every year, looking at a clock to find out the time is beyond him. He simply cannot do it. For me, the combination of being able to keep erratic work hours along with the benefit of being surrounded by people just as peculiar as I am, serves as a type of social camouflage, allowing my weirdness to blend with the rest.

Unlike my A.D.D. Lex Luthor brain, my day-to-day mind is all Clark Kent, casually imitating the work habits of other humans. Even better, occasionally my Clark Kent mind pulls off his glasses and, suddenly super, can hyper-focus for 14 hours straight, several days in a row. In those marathon stints, Supermind can accomplish far more than mere mortals in the same amount of time. Then, after those freakishly productive super days, something unrelated will cause stress, anger, or some other intense emotion. That burst of emotion makes my A.D.D. go all Lex Luthor again, eventually dropping a Kryptonite anvil the size of Texas on Supermind. Since Supermind was concentrating on my job, he didn't see that coming at all so he's suddenly in a big-ass super-coma. Then, whoever is running the show up there doesn't know what to do since Supermind is out cold. Panicked, they send in Bizarro Stupidmind to fill in.

Bizarro Stupidmind—a barely functioning moron whose initials are appropriately B.S.—goes through the motions but doesn't really do anything. If something is needed in a hurry, do not under any circumstances pressure Bizarro Stupidmind because he'll drag my ass under my desk for a 20-minute nap before you can say, "Urgent!"

Eventually though, Clark Kent sidles back in, sends Bizarro Stupidmind home, and we are back to generally human-level work. Then, at varying intervals, this cycle repeats. To date, I've managed to keep everyone's identities secret. Still, it makes for some very awkward moments when someone shows up expecting Supermind and instead they get B.S. This makes my being a single parent and college professor an adventure for everyone involved.

Ironically, when I was a college student, I used to wonder why college professors were such an eccentric group. Even if someone had pulled me aside at that time and explained about rebooting naps or the periodic inability to comprehend email, I still wouldn't have gotten it, not really. As an undergraduate, there were many things I didn't understand. Partly, that was because I was pretty drunk for a large portion of those years. Likely the prolonged inebriation was also why I didn't realize I had A.D.D. I did not make that discovery until I was single-parenting my way through my seven years of graduate school when the stakes were nice and high.

Not only were the stakes high, but so were my expectations of myself - as a graduate student, as a newly-divorced parent of twins, and as a person. My expectations left no margin for error in my life. During my Ph.D., there was virtually no time for anything beyond my responsibilities. For years, I could feel my own sanity precariously perched. I knew making one wrong move would bring down my entire, carefully scheduled life.

Like most people, I couldn't afford to be a student without an income. In order to pay bills and fund my twin's extracurricular activities, I taught undergraduate courses while I was a graduate student. One class I taught was a building design studio course.

The supervising professor—who helped the Ph.D. students instructing these studios learn to teach as they went along—used to say with a flourish of his slender hand, "Remember, presentation drawings shouldn't fill the entire page. Drawings are like life, you don't want to fill every inch of it. There should be margins, white space for the eyes to rest."

While appreciating both the design and life wisdom in leaving space to pause and rest, this wasn't a period of my life in which I was able to make that happen.

For those four years, I started each day at 4:30 A.M. Getting up in the quiet darkness provided an opportunity to work on my dissertation research in peace before parenting duties started at 6:30.

"Mommy, I can't find my shoes."

"I put them next to your backpack."

"Not *those* shoes," said Avery with her loose strawberry-blond curls tapping her cheeks as she shook her head. "I want the sparkly ones, with the strappies."

"You have gym today, sweetheart."

"Mommy, Avery likes a boy," reported Beck.

"What? Avery, you need to eat your pancakes."

"She does, I saw her standing all close to Bradley in line."

"So," said Avery, "I wanted to kiss him."

"Wait, what happened?" I asked.

Sitting down her fork, Avery stood up and said, "Well, we were in line at the drinking fountain and I scooted up real close to him," mimicking the movement of moving closer to someone. "And I thought: this is a pretty good start."

I grinned, "Wait, did Bradley want you to kiss him?"

Looking thoughtful, Avery said, "Um, no."

"Well, hmm. Here's the thing, you are not really supposed to be kissing people at school even if they do want you to kiss them."

Avery huffed, "Well, where am I supposed to kiss him then?"

"Hmmm, that really wasn't my point…" I started.

Avery interrupted, "Hey mom, can Bradley come over for a play date?"

I raised my eyebrows. Beck shrugged and through a mouth full of pancake said, "See, mom, I told you."

After dropping the twins off at elementary school, I'd go to the University to alternate between being a student in some classes and teaching others. Since each day's schedule was tightly packed, I kept my textbooks in my car. That way, if I arrived some place a few minutes early, I could spend those moments productively catching up on reading assignments. Without leftover time or energy, this delicate balance could easily be shaken if something didn't go as planned. With that, I lived with the constant stress of knowing mine was a life on the edge, with everything at risk of collapse from the slightest breeze. The only reprieve was the quiet peace I found during the 30-minute run I took each morning.

Throughout and since graduate school, people asked me, "Sloane, how are you doing all this?"

My standard response was an honest one, "I have no idea. I'm pretty sure I'm just one fetal position away from losing my mind."

It wasn't all bad, though. Often life's high-speed momentum disguised my mind's tendency for distraction and running-off in unpredictable directions. When it came to relationships, this meant the unpredictable party in my mind was not the same liability it was with my work. The only exception was Bizarro Stupidmind's inability to problem solve in a crisis. So, some days I was the hero saving the day but, on an A.D.D. day, I was the damsel in distress. From deep within, I despised my inner damsel. She was completely at odds with my vision of myself.

I was a single parent, a Ph.D. student, and a runner. I could write about research before the sun came up, get the twins off to elementary school along with allergen-free cupcakes to share with their class, and still get a 3-mile run in before getting to campus by 9 A.M. I was the Swiss Army knife of humans— small, compact, and useful in so many situations. Even so, this weakness—this inability to always be self-sufficient—haunted me. My greatest fear was coming to depend upon someone and then, someday, that person not being there when I needed them the most.

This was both the appeal and the hazard of having a relationship with the most dependable human I knew, David. He worked in the building industry which was refreshing. For a change, I did not have to discuss research socially. For me, research was like a sedated Disney World—a fun place to visit but I didn't want to live there.

Since David's job was one he did well and had been doing for some time, he approached work with a practiced comfort. In part, David's ease with work as well as life was because he had one of those amazing dispositions that simply was not programmed for worry. He had a comfortable balance in life that I'd never managed to make for myself. For instance, his strong work ethic was counterbalanced by his free time spent performing in community theater, oftentimes with his sons alongside him.

So, I'd marvel as David marched through life doing what needed to be done but not feeling he was responsible for controlling every little life outcome. He was lighthearted and free from the stress that comes with the relentless pursuit of perfection. Even without the pressure of perfectionism, still David's life had plenty of things to cause stress. For instance, he single-parented his two sons who lived with him most of the time. Rather than agonizing over each detail ahead of time, he woke up each morning, got his kids off to school, and went to work, comfortable in his belief each day would work itself out.

Not only was his calm but cheerful demeanor refreshing, he was the most intrinsically capable man I knew. A few weeks after I met David, I was driving my son and daughter home from school when my car got stuck in the snow. Having recently moved to this far-flung part of the Midwest for graduate school, Wisconsin's frigid climate and massive snowfalls were new to me. So, I was completely unprepared when my car was suddenly lodged in a roadside snowbank. With two five-year-olds in the car and knee-deep snow blanketing the ground, striking out on foot was not an option. With only a few months of living in this region which I was quickly learning was one-part dairy farm—one-part Princess Elsa having a mood-swing, I did not have even a single person—family or friend—in the area whom I could call for help. David was the only person I knew at all, having been on two dates with him.

Since I was hyper-focused on earning my way into a professorship, I had no intention of dating during graduate school. My primary focus was building up my credentials. In the pursuit of that goal, I accepted an invitation to be on a 4-person panel discussing the connection between health and building design for a construction management conference—a conference that David happened to be attending. Although I didn't know whether he was attracted by my insightful comments or the fact I was one of the few people at the conference who did not have a penis, David introduced himself to me after the panel discussion.

"Hi Dr. Noah," said this man, with dark hair and gray eyes that sparkled with the light.

"Actually, I'm not a doctor yet," I explained.

"Even so, almost-Dr.-Noah," David said, "I thought what you said about sustainable design being just as important for people's health as it is for the planet was really interesting. Could we have lunch tomorrow so you can tell me more about that?"

"Oh, um, well, tomorrow is Saturday," I started, thinking there must be some reason I couldn't. Realizing the twins would be at their dad's and coming up blank when trying to find other obstacles to prevent it, "Okay, I don't take long breaks, though, but I could meet you at Marvin's at noon."

"You bet," smiled David. And he was off before I could give it a second thought.

That lunch date was followed shortly thereafter with a dinner date set on the pretense that we still needed to finish the conversation started at lunch. Based on those two get-togethers with David, I was still on the fence about whether I thought there was relationship potential there or not. While stuck in the snow, I pushed my reservations aside as I realized David was the only local person for whom I had a phone number. Without any other options, I hesitantly dialed his work number from my cell phone.

When he answered his office phone, I said, "So, I know we don't know each other that well, but what are your feelings about helping damsels in distress?"

David laughed, "Do you need to be rescued, milady?"

After I explained my twins and I were in the car and stuck in the snow alongside the road, he asked, "Do you have a snow shovel?" When I told him I didn't, he said, "Well, give me an extra ten minutes to stop and buy one. I should be there in about twenty minutes."

Then he left his office, bought a snow shovel and a couple bags of salt, then rescued my sorry ass.
I was used to struggling through things on my own. Despite that, the sheer relief that came with, just this one time, knowing there was someone who was happy to step-in to help felt nothing short of miraculous. From that point, our acquaintance started evolving into a partnership.

Since we both worked in the building and design field—I on the design side and he on the construction side—our interests and hobbies overlapped enough for us to find common ground. Even more importantly, we had similar senses of humor. Consequently, David and I could have more fun on a Sunday afternoon at Home Depot than most couples could being out on the town on Saturday night. One such Sunday, we pulled into my driveway with David's trunk full of Home Depot purchases.

As we got out of his black SUV and walked around towards the tailgate, I said, "I really like those two flower pots I bought. Unfortunately, it will probably take me six months before I get around to drilling holes in the bottoms."

"Oh, you need holes in them?" asked David as he opened the tailgate.

"Well, only if I want to be able to keep plants alive in them," I answered.

Smiling, he pulled a red Milwaukee tool case towards the open end of the trunk. In a fluid movement, he clicked open the case, pulled out a red and black drill, and after a brief *rizzz, rizzz* sound, each flower pot had a freshly drilled hole in the bottom.

For David, it was instinct to pitch in when something needed to be done. This natural tendency combined with his being capable and at ease with power tools was as striking to me as it was ordinary for him. In the academic world I inhabited, men were valued for their ideas and research skills but very few of those I knew even owned power tools.

After putting one flower pot inside the other, he handed the stack to me and said, "There you go, babe."

To David, his action was reflexive and didn't warrant a second thought. By contrast, I found myself suddenly in the presence of an exotic male specimen who not only was good with his hands and kept a cordless drill in his trunk but also naturally participated in mundane household tasks. This was more than a wonder; this was soft porn for women. Letting David sit the flower pots in my hands, I put them back into the trunk.

Then looking him in the eye, I said, "Upstairs. My room. Now."

"As you wish," he said with a wink as I pulled him into the house.

# Monster in My Head

## Chapter 2

David was not a man of many words, but he had a superpower—an ability to always show up. His easy-going nature enabled him to set aside whatever he was doing and participate in life, even when things arose unexpectedly. He was never too busy, too distracted, nor was this just a show he put on to try to impress someone he wanted to date.

For instance, three years into our relationship on a Tuesday afternoon in graduate school, I was stubbornly trying to pound out broken thoughts on my laptop keyboard against the resistance of Bizarro Stupidmind. I typed a couple of sentences, deleted those. Wrote several new sentences, deleted those. My thoughts were awkward, incomplete, and not, well, something a smart person would write.

I typed, "Something smart. Something insightful. Something useful. Please? PLEASSSSSSSEEEEEEEE!!!!!!!"

*Coffee,* I thought. *I need more coffee. Yes, and I need it in my "You got this" mug.* With that thought, I jolted up from the sofa and my open computer leapt from my lap, clapping explosively onto the floor. Frozen, my wide eyes stared at the laptop now making an upside down "V" on the floor. Research data, over 170 pages of dissertation text, thousands of hours of work all lived inside that black machine pointing at me, butt-first. Before I could move, I thought the unthinkable: *What if it is all gone? What if I just destroyed everything I'd done for the past 3.5 years? Sure, I had a few stray files backed up, but I couldn't remember the last time I'd backed up my dissertation. Oh God.*

Slowly I bent down and turned over the laptop like it was a small, injured animal. The screen—now dark—had web-like cracks veining the entire glass face. I couldn't think of what to do next. I waited for an idea, cradling the machine's corpse in my arms. When it was clear I could not resolve this on my own, I called David.

Silently, I despised myself for the gratitude I felt when I heard David's voice, "Hello?"

"I think I just killed my dissertation; I mean, my laptop. I think it's really dead. The screen's obliterated and it won't turn on. It fell. It fell when I dropped it. I, I, I can't…I don't know. I need you to find out. Take it and see. I don't know if my dissertation, all my work, is still there."

"Be right over," said David.

Just as my shoulders relaxed, my relief was erased by guilt. *I shouldn't depend on other people to fix my problems. What if I came to rely on David, or anyone really, and then one day they were no longer there? Then what? It would be like when I was married to Tom—who was never there for me when I needed him most.*

*After years of incorrectly assuming Tom would come through when needed, disappointment after disappointment compounded heavily. Eventually, I realized it was safer not to expect help from anyone at all rather than face the continual sting of being assured help would be there yet when need came, I was alone with nothing but my false hopes for company. Someday I might really, really need David and he might not come. It would be the whole silk bedding incident all over again.* Still, with the A.D.D. cloud pressing me and the laptop's digital carcass in my hands, this left little room for independence and self-sufficiency ideals. So again, I risked trusting David.

Every time I'd open the door to him, he'd be standing there, half turned away. With my "Hello," he'd turn toward me slowly, all crooked smile and sparkling eyes, and the speed of life eased. Hurry wasn't in him. With him, problems were not so frightening because they came at a walk instead of a run. Whatever swirling I was caught in, it would be handled and handled well - but at an easy cadence. When David was around, it was as though the Universe was required to march to David's rhythm. Once David would walk back out the door, though, I'd be swept up into the next hurricane that came along.

While I knew I was already stretched holding the edges of my life together, still my tendency was to fling myself from one overly-ambitious goal to the next without acknowledging there may be limits to what I could or should do. Like a deranged howler monkey swinging from vine-to-vine, I hurdled through life. In this mad momentum, one semester I took-on a freelance writing job to bring in extra money. Not only was it a dull project which entailed going through the company's archives to put together a thorough corporate history but also, I did not know how I might accommodate anything more within my packed schedule. Even so, I ignored the small voice in my head that said, "Hey lady, when the hell do you think you are going to be able to write a book?"

To accommodate the project, my schedule shifted. Rather than days starting at 4:30 A.M., they now started at 3:45 A.M. In addition to that, any other crevice of time in my life was filled with the book project.

In the end, I completed the book by the company's deadline but this came at a high personal price. With the added stress serving as a sizable final straw of sorts, my tendency toward worry evolved into clinical anxiety. In coping with this newly acquired, relentless fear raging within me, my tolerance for outside stimuli like sound from a TV show or background conversation in a busy restaurant was more than my raw nerves could bear. Without hesitation or needing to be asked, David adjusted. Rather than picking me up at the university to go out for lunch which was our habit, he started a new routine. He stopped for take-out before coming to pick me up then we'd drive to a quiet corner in a wooded park. There, surrounded by nothing but the sound of wind through the trees and the skittering of small animals, we'd eat our lunch with a side of low-key conversation. Being with David was like exhaling.

By contrast, on my own I felt I was holding my breath as I struggled to cope with a now unbearably irritating world. After getting Avery and Beck off to their dad's house for the weekend, I came home, curled into a tight ball on my un-made bed, and for hours shook with tears. That's what my life was then: I white-knuckled it through my responsibilities then promptly collapsed into a soggy puddle.

Soon after my eyes stung, rubbed raw from the stream of tears, I jumped, startled with my phone's buzz. At first, I didn't move but quickly decided I couldn't stand to hear the phone buzz a second time. Through red, swollen eyes, I read a text message from David.

"Do you want to go to the wine bar for dinner?"

It sounded impossible. I wasn't fit to be around people. I answered, "I don't feel good."

"I'll be there in a few minutes," David responded.

I was still curled in a ball on my bed when I heard David walk into my room.

"Hey beautiful, I'm going to cuddle you."

I nodded, with my back still towards David. As David slipped into my bed beside me, I uncurled myself enough to let him spoon me.

With one arm securely around my waist, he pulled me tight against him and murmured, "I'm here."

I felt my shoulders relax and my breaths slowed.

Encouraged by my relaxing body, David's fingers found their way under my sweatshirt and skimmed my stomach.

"You have the softest skin," he whispered into my ear, as his fingertips glided upward to lightly trace one of my nipples.

I hoped the early evening's gray light, that dimly lit my bedroom, would mask my red face as I turned to face him.

"I missed you so much today," he said as his palm made its way back down my side and rested on my waist.

My anxiety, a terrifying monster living in my mind, kept my body as well as my mind tied in knots when it was left to its own devices. Somehow, intuitively understanding this, David never tried to wrestle the monster with words or logic. Instead he soothed my body with touch. And to my continual surprise, the monster couldn't rage once my body relaxed.

From my waist, his hand glided along my thigh, eventually draping it across his hip. As I looked up at David from under damp eyelashes, he took my face in his hands and he kissed me gently.

In a breathy voice, David said, "We are over-dressed for this party, Sloane." Then, leaning away from me, he pulled my sweatshirt over my head. Following, the rest of our clothing found its way onto the floor. He kissed me again, but more deeply. I could feel David was already hard.

Despite the hunger in his eyes, he lifted my back with a slow and gentle strength, moving me further from the bed's edge. His tender patience sparked an urgent ache in me. Now, without our clothes between us, he pulled me closer, until there was no distance between us.

"Good God almighty," I whispered as he entered me.

Month-by-month, the anxiety slowly burned itself out. That's when I found myself shocked by another unexpected challenge. During the winter before my graduation the following May, David was diagnosed with an aggressive case of prostate cancer. After getting this news under the green light of a doctor's exam room, David drove straight to my house.

With a stony face and calm voice, he relayed the doctor's words to me, "I need to deal with it immediately because it's going to get worse quickly."

"What does that mean—to deal with it?"

"It means I have to get my prostate removed in just over a week."

When he saw my eyes fill with tears, he kissed me on the cheek.

"What does that mean for you?"

"Well, it will probably keep me alive, but it may mean I can't..." David's words faded into silence.

"Oh babe, I'm so, so sorry this is happening."

David took a deep breath and squared his shoulders, "Yeah, well, it is what it is. I just need to get away, to think. I'm headed to the cabin for a few days."

"Ok, yes, let's go to the cabin," I said.

"No, Sloane. I need it to just be me."

"But..." I started then David cut me off.

"I just need to be alone. I will stop by as soon as I get back," he said, kissing my furrowed brow.

For the next three days, David went camping alone, while I worried. *Should I let him be on his own after hearing such life-shaking news?* I wondered. Rather than chasing after someone I wasn't sure wanted to be chased, though, I asked my long-time therapist, Dr. B., about it.

"When faced with a life-threatening illness, some people prefer to be surrounded by the people they love. Others prefer solitude. If David needs to retreat to process all this, then it is okay to let him do that," said Dr. B.

With that, David retreated while I waited. When David returned from his cabin, his peaceful nature returned with him. He walked back into my house and smiled as the twins rushed toward him to share their latest project, a comic book they were creating. Apparently, David's earlier introduction of his childhood love of comic books had taken root in Avery and Beck. David paused then, fueled by their excitement and flipped through the stapled pages and admired their work.

"Fantastic! I can't wait to find out how it ends!" David exclaimed.

Looking proud and happy, the twins' smiles quickly turned into wrinkled noses as David kissed me.

"Gross," said Beck. "Let's go finish our comic, Avery."

So it was that David acknowledged his cancer, did what was needed, and moved forward without complaint.

Shortly before his prostate removal surgery, I asked him if he was afraid.

"Do you mean afraid of dying?" he asked.

I nodded.

"Nah, not really," he said. Then with a crooked grin, he added, "I am scared I won't be able to get it up anymore though."

Now it was my turn to be there for him.

Since both of us were well-acquainted with life's tendency toward complications and obstacles—whether clinical anxiety or cancer—we walked through these as a team seamlessly.  As we moved forward together, we tried to ignore the end of my Ph.D. program looming only months away. For me, the idea of finishing graduate school was bittersweet. In large part, I was thrilled to earn the degree that would put an end to years of getting up hours before the sun. Additionally, the idea I would soon have a job with a decent salary was hugely alluring. Even so, I didn't want the "us" that was David and me to end. I wanted to keep our relationship exactly as it was: he single-parenting at his house and me single-parenting at mine but with us still walking through life as a unit, our own little army of two. Despite my wishes on the matter, time changes life and we had no choice but to change in response.

That's when David first brought up marriage. Although he introduced the idea causally, he laughed at the look the topic brought to my face. He later described my expression as more closely resembling someone who thought they were about to be murdered rather than someone who was receiving an informal marriage proposal. Following his casual but emotional appeal, he switched to logic.

"We have been dating 3 ½ years. Most women start looking at engagement rings six months in," he said.

"Yeah, I'm not like that," I said.

David smiled, "No, you're not. You're the emotional equivalent of a glacier."

"Meaning I'm cold?" I asked with raised eyebrows.

With a laugh, David said, "No, quite the opposite. You just move very slowly when it comes to commitment."

"Glaciers have to move slowly because their presence changes the landscape forever," I said. "When I'm ready to move toward more commitment, there will be no stopping me. I'm just not there yet."

Taking both of my hands in his, David said, "God, your hands are shaking just discussing this."

I explained, "The idea of getting married again scares the Frappuccino out of me. When I was married, I tried so hard and, still, it failed miserably. Taking that risk again facing a possible failure that I can't prevent - I just can't do it. I can't ."

Suddenly, it was graduation and a tenure track university job waited for me in Florida.

"But I can't just let you leave," said David.

"I don't see that we have any other choice," I said.

"Then I will move with you."

"How? How would that even work? Your ex isn't going to let you just take off with the boys."

"Then I will move to Florida and visit them as much as I can."

"You can't just leave behind your sons. They'd resent me. You'd resent me. Hell, I'd resent me—I just can't be that person," I explained.

"I think I could make it work," said David.

"It would be very selfish of us. I just can't, in good conscience, be a part of that. Every time your sons said they missed you, I'd feel guilty. Plus, they need you. You need to teach them how to be good men."

David's shoulders slumped. "But I want to be with you. Don't you want this? Me?"

"I do. I do, but what if..."

"What if?" David echoed, eyebrows drawn tight.

"It's just too complicated right now."

"It's not that complicated for me. For me you are the answer to every question."

There was a pause.

"It's not the same for you, is it? Am I not enough?" David asked quietly.

Then a louder pause.

"Yes. No. I don't know. I just can't make that call right now."

David looked stunned, like I had punched him.

Then the only option left to keep our relationship going was to accept five or more years of long-distance dating. Since that seemed like just a way of just delaying an inevitable break up, no conclusion was drawn, no agreement was made. We just stopped talking about it then held on until time separated us.

Then one July morning, David carried my suitcases to my car, leaving my house empty. After putting our bags into the trunk, David wrapped his arms around me, tightly.

"Hey David, mom said we can get a dog after we move to Florida!" spouted Avery.

"Great. That's great, sweetheart," he said with forced enthusiasm.

Before climbing into the backseat, each of my twins paused in turn to add their own hug to mine and David's.

"Bye, David!"

"Miss you! Love you!"

"And Avery and Beck, I miss and love you, too, right back," said David, removing one of his arms from my back to return each of the twins' hugs.

Then my son and daughter climbed into the backseat chirping away at one another. David and I kissed our goodbyes, faces wet from tears. If there were words to say, we couldn't find them. Pulling me into an even tighter embrace, David kissed me once more. Then, suddenly surrendering me, he stepped back to let me get into the driver's seat. Closing the door, I started the car. Putting the car into reverse, I looked over toward David and waved my fingers weakly as the car started moving. David lifted his hand in response then dropped it quickly, as though its weight was too much.

Trying to ignore the impulse to put the car into park and run back to David, I said to the twins, "Hey I got something for us to listen to during the long drive to Florida. I bought the Harry Potter audio books!"

The twins clapped and cheered as I turned on the car's CD player. I could feel David's eyes watching us as we drove away. Even so, I kept my eyes on the road ahead.

# A Few Good Men

## Chapter 3

Heartbroken but hopeful, I threw myself into my work in Florida. There my life was a constant stream of academic work interlaced with packing school lunches and attending elementary school band concerts. With life's effusive current, I hardly noticed the months then years ticking by.

Then, one Thursday afternoon as I pulled out of my ex-husband's driveway, I answered a call from Nolan, my best friend.

"Please say you just dropped off the twins at their dad's," said Nolan.

"You are correct, ma'am."

"Gross, don't 'ma'am' me. It makes is sound like I'm a mom."

"Nolan, you are a mom."

"Okay, then it makes me sound like I'm MY mom."

"Fair enough. What's up?"

"The bottoms' of our glasses, chica! Come have $3.00 margaritas with us, pronto! Am putting you on speaker."

As the background noise over the phone became louder, I said, "I'm assuming that means Sean and Peter are there too?" Since Sean and Peter were a couple in addition to being our closest friends, generally Nolan and I mostly referred to them affectionately as "our best gays."

"Gay men talking," said Peter, by way of a greeting.

While Sean, a surgical nurse, was born and raised in Florida, Peter, an architecture professor, who grew up in Kentucky. Even so, Peter spent 12 years in New York City prior to moving south again. This time in the Northeast noticeably altered Peter's speech. While Peter's words still dripped with his Kentucky drawl, he delivered them at a faster, more northern speed. He sounded like an over-educated Jeff Foxworthy needing a double-dose of Ritalin.

"Oh hon-ey these margaritas are not going to drink themselves! How fast can you be here?" asked Peter.

As I pulled open its glass door, I stepped into what was a teal, orange, and red swirl of noise—silverware clanking against plates, voices, and Mariachi music struggling to be heard. I waved a hand at the hostess as I walked by.

With a nod of her head, the hostess mouthed, "Bar?"

I confirmed with my own nod.

Upon entering the side room, home to the restaurant's bar sheltered by its own faux roof with clay mission tiles overhead, I could already hear Peter's voice over the noise in the busy restaurant.

"I'm telling ya'll its genius—not Brittney Spears performing 'Toxic' genius—but still genius!

I saw Sean first since his mocha-colored bald head was almost always a full head-height above everyone else's.

"Hey kids," I said as I reached them.

"We ordered drinks," said Sean, motioning toward the table.

Other than a couple papers pushed off to the side, the table held frozen margaritas of varying colors, grouped in threes in front of each person as well as in front of the empty chair which was presumably for me.

"Are we celebrating something?" I asked.

"Naturally," answered Sean. "We Botoxed today, you know, as preventive medicine."

"I thought you two were looking unnaturally youthful," I said.

Tilting his face up toward the light hanging overhead, then turning it slowly from side-to-side, Peter said, "By youthful do you mean 90210 Luke Perry youthful or Riverdale Luke Perry?

I started to answer, but Sean interrupted, "Keep in mind if you say Riverdale Luke Perry, Peter is likely to spear you with one of these little toothpick umbrellas."

"Sit Sloane!" said Nolan.

As I sat in the empty chair, Peter said with a frown, "Sloane, we have a mission for you."

"If I choose to accept it?"

Then Peter's face brightened, "Oh sweetie, no! You absolutely do not get a choice in this!"

I looked at Nolan to see if I should be worried. Nolan just shrugged indicating that nothing could be done about it even if I should be worried.

Sean cleared his throat then said in his big, deep voice, "For the official record, Nolan, please state exactly how many dates Sloane has been on in the last month."

"Zero."

"How about in the last year?"

"Zero."

In the last two years?"

"That'd still be zero."

"I thought we covered this," I huffed, "I'm too busy."

"Oh yes, yes, woman, you have been professor-ing like crazy. But enough already!" said Peter.

"After 730 days of celibacy, it is no longer up for debate. You are going to start online dating," explained Sean.

"I'm *not* doing online dating."

"Hon-ey, unless your vagina is on sabbatical, there is no legitimate reason for this extended vacancy.

"Nolan, tell her," said Sean.

"You're doing online dating," said Nolan.

"I'm not going to take the time to set up a dating profile."

"Absolutely, darlin'! That's why we already set it up for you! It's going to be fab'! You have a happy hour date tomorrow and a brunch date on Saturday."

"Please say you're kidding," I pleaded.

"Oh, Peter never kids about mating season!" said Sean, grinning with one eyebrow raised.

"Cause ya'll, it's springtime and love is in the air!" Peter proclaimed throwing his hands upward.

"I think it's time! Let's meet the contestants, shall we," said Nolan, as she flipped over the first paper from near the table's edge.

I looked down. On it was a picture of a man who looked about the same age as my graduate students.

Nolan explained, "This is Ryan. He's 26 and does something in computers. He likes doing Cross-Fit and watching action movies.

"He's 26? But I'm...I'm just a few years older than that," I said.

"Young is good," explained Peter, patting my hand. "Think of young guys as the veal of the dating world!"

Nolan turned over the next sheet of paper which showed a man notably older than the one before with sandy brown hair and glasses, Peter said, "This is Simon, 42 years old, bank vice president, collects wine."

"I don't think..." I started but Peter brushed my comment aside.

"So, what are you going to wear?" asked Sean excitedly.

Flustered, I paused then said, "I don't know. Something like this, I guess," motioning toward my outfit.

"Gray skirt, white button up, blue blazer, string of pearls, flats..." reported Sean, with a crinkled brow.

"Hon-ey, no, no, no! These are dates! You are not running for president of the PTA!" said Peter.

"But no worries, my friend! We bought you a present, just in case," said Nolan as, on cue, Sean pulled a sturdy black, rectangular box from underneath his chair.

Accepting the box from Sean, I said, "Um, it's from Saks Fifth Avenue," as I read the box's label.

"Well, we were going to shop at JC Penny's, then we remembered that we are not hobos," said Sean who had a notorious love of fine things.

As I slid off the top of the box, Sean commentated, "To make your debut back into the dating world, you need the appropriate costuming, so we are starting with this."

With both hands, I gently lifted a strappy, black mini-dress tucked neatly within crisp tissue paper within the box.

"I have bras with more fabric than this," I said, furrowing my brow.

Nolan said, "It will be beautiful on you! I tried it on to make sure it would fit."

Sean added, "Then after tonight's fiesta, we reconvene tomorrow at Coffee Culture for the date debriefing."

"Yes, at 1500 hours," confirmed Nolan. As a civilian working for the U.S. Airforce, Nolan commonly used military time.

When 1500 hours came, I arrived at Coffee Culture, a quirky coffee shop laid out in a small, turn-of-the-century cottage. Inside, Nolan and our best gays were already waiting for me at a corner table, near the white-painted brick fireplace.

"Yoga pants and a hoodie? Way to get dressed up for us, Sloane," said Sean in a dead-pan voice.

I frowned at him then sat in the black bentwood café chair in front of the spare cup of coffee resting on the petite tabletop.

"So? How were they?" said Nolan with one elbow on the table and her chin resting in her palm.

"Yeah, how was the Veal?" asked Sean. "He's so hot! Isn't he?"

"The Veal? Yes, Ryan 'the Veal' was very hot," I reported.

"And how was the wine bar?" asked Nolan.

"Well it was a beautiful evening with just a light breeze so we decided to sit at one of the bar's courtyard tables," I shared.

"Nice," encouraged Sean.

"Matter-of-fact, I even found myself thinking, 'Okay, maybe this will be fun,'" I said.

"So, tell us, tell us! How fun was it?" chirped Peter.

"Well, first, the world's youngest cocktail waitress came to take our order. After we told her what we'd like to drink, the waitress asked the Veal for his I.D. As she looked as his license, I started to get mine out as well. When I tried to hand it to her, she waved me off and said, 'Oh, you're fine. I don't need to see yours.'"

"Ouch!" said Nolan following a wince.

"Still, you can come back from that," suggested Sean.

"So, a little while later we noticed another waitress, waiting on a nearby table. Glancing toward her, the Veal said, 'Wow, that hair color is one that does not occur in nature.' Now keep in mind here, I was nervous and thus sucking down glasses of Chardonnay one after the next."

"Oh no! What did you say, Sloane?" asked Nolan.

"I said, 'Yeah, you just know the carpet doesn't match those drapes.'"

"Okay, moderately witty," commented Peter, nodding his head.

"Oh no! NO! Because then the Veal said, 'I don't know what you mean.'"

"Huh? How could he have not heard that before?" asked Nolan.

"I couldn't figure it out either, so I went ahead and explained that the drapes referred to the hair on her head and the carpet was, well, located in the hoo-ha vicinity."

Cocking his head to the side, Sean, wondering where this was going, said, "Okay...."

"Then the Veal said, 'Oh, I've never been with a woman with pubic hair.'"

The three of them stared back at me blankly.

"I know, right?! Then I asked him how that was possible, and the Veal said, 'Every woman I've ever gone to bed with shaves it all off.'"

"Oh no," moaned Nolan, "It's his age."

"Exactly! Apparently, people under 30 have collectively decided to be hairless and there I sat, with my gigantic National Geographic bush, desperately trying to change the subject."

"Oh honey," said Peter through laughter, "You don't shave at all?"

"Well sure, but just your regular housekeeping, not full on removal!"

"So, what did you do?" asked Sean.

"First, all I could think was this guy was probably watching Teenage Mutant Ninja Turtles when I went off to college. After that, I just downed the rest of that glass of wine and got the hell out of there!"

Trying to stifle his laughs, Sean said, "I bet brunch was better then."

"Yes, brunch. How could it be worse, ya know?"

Sean nodded.

"So, I sat down with Banker Boy, and Simon says…"

"Ha, 'Simon says'!" said Nolan.

I smiled fleetingly then pushed on, "Simon was good with the small talk. We chatted about our kids and the activities they are involved in. It was all very light and friendly."

"That sounds promising in a rated 'G' kind of way," said Sean.

"And then about 45 minutes in, with his croissant still in his hand, Banker-boy asks if after brunch, I'd like to go back to his place and have sex!"

"Oh Lordy!" said Peter, shaking his head.

"Since I was still trying to keep it light-hearted, I said, 'As a general rule, I don't sleep with someone until I can at least spell their last name."

"To which he responded…" prompted Nolan.

"S-c-h-u-m-a-c-h-e-r!"

Over the sudden burst of laughter, I had to raise my voice say, "So I made up some excuse and bolted as quickly as I could."

Peter, still laughing, said, "It will get better, sweetie."

"No. No way! I just can't! I cannot date under these conditions!"

For some months after that, Nolan and our best gays dropped the subject of dating. That's why they all sat wide-eyed when I told them over a different cup of coffee on a sunny Sunday afternoon, that I'd gone on a lunch date that week.

"What's this?!" asked Nolan in surprise.

"And who might this young stallion be?" asked Peter.

"I think you know him, Peter. He works at the University too. It's Eduardo, that professor in Urban Planning."

"Oooo, that fresh-faced little tamale! He's a hot one!" said Peter.

"And that accent! Hottest. Thing. Ever," I agreed.

"So how was lunch with him?" asked Peter.

"Well," I started with a grin, "at first we talked about research then down-shifted into talking about our hobbies. That's about when, he casually grazed my arm with his fingers and said he'd love to teach me to Salsa dance."

"Oh, he is so yummy!" gushed Peter.

"I know! I was putty at that point! Then as lunch wrapped up and he said something about his kids, so I asked how long he's been divorced from their mother. Then, in that breathtaking accent, he said, 'Oh bella dama…'"

"Oh no, no, Sloane. Don't do the accent," said Sean, wrinkling his nose.

"Fine," I said. "He said he wasn't divorced but he and his wife had an understanding."

"Oh yikes, that's so not your style!" said Nolan.

"Did you run away again?" asked Sean.

"Not this time, sir."

"Oh, my Lord! You decided to have an affair with him? Now this is getting interesting!" said Peter, rubbing his hands together.

"No, not that either. I just thanked him for lunch, told him I enjoyed the conversation, but I don't want to be someone's b-string. If I'm not the starting line-up, for me, it's just not worth playing."

There was a pause followed by Nolan soothing, "You did the right thing."

Slowly, Peter shook his head. Then in a tone of dismay he said, "Wow. I cannot believe you didn't hit that."

# Naked Fortune Telling
## Chapter 4

By summer, I could no longer stand the idea of going out on dates to get to know people who were essentially strangers. I wanted consistency and comfort. With that, I could think of nothing or no one more consistent and comforting than David, my partner during graduate school.

Under the pretense of checking on his health, I picked up my phone and called him.

When I asked how he was, he responded, "I'm really good, actually. The cancer is still detectable in my blood, but it seems to be staying stagnant. The doc says it's not going to be a problem unless there is a change."

"That's great. That's really, really great," I said. "What have you been up to?"

"Oh, well, the boys and just played rolls in a local production of "Finian's Rainbow.""

Then we were off talking work, kids, and eventually reminiscing.

Three years before, we had left behind something that was still smoldering. With this new conversational fuel to serve as kindling, what there was between us reignited. As he told me about his youngest son, now in high school, I felt differently than before. It no longer felt like such an impossibly long time until we could make decisions without hinging them on the needs of our children. To my surprise, I found I wanted David again now, even if it meant dating long-distance for a year or two more.

Still, I needed to find out if he was 'with' anyone. In an effort at nonchalance, one evening I started a text conversation about moving for work. Would he, I asked, consider relocating for his career? When he said he wasn't sure, I asked if he had a partner, thinking perhaps this explained his answer.

"No, there's no partner. I was just thinking about the Chris. It's not very practical to move until he is older," he wrote.

Startled by my own relief, I thought, *Wow, I really am ready to get back together.* He explained he tried dating a few times, but with limited sexual function after having his prostate removed, these romantic relationships ended quickly. From conversations years before, I knew he hoped to get 'the equipment' functioning via an obscenely expensive surgery. Since some insurance companies did not cover it, likely it did not nor would not come easily or cheaply. Even so, those memories of our eight post-surgery months together were happy ones. Then I made up my mind: regardless of where he was with that surgery, I wanted to make a go of it with him.

Still, memories are not always dependable. Time's effects can be tricky. Occasionally, time polishes memories, making them shinier than reality. In other instances, memories pale as months and years pass, slowly degrading their potency. For me, my memories of David and I had not faded at all. Matter-of-fact, I worried these crisp images might be honed beyond the fineness of actual experience.   Although I knew what and who I wanted, a persisting anxiety troubled me. Would the reality of a reunion with David match the intense, memory-laced expectations I'd created? Was my recollection of our time together accurate, or was nostalgia veiling the truth? If I spent time with him, touching him and seeing his face when I talked to him, would I find my lovely memories dampened by reality? I really didn't think so. Still, I needed to be sure.

This time, I didn't call David first, though. Instead, I called Nolan.

"Nolan, I'm still in love with David," I said.

"Interesting," responded Nolan. "And what are you thinking you will do about this new realization?"

"I just need to see him to make sure I haven't built everything up in my head. I'm in such a different emotional place than I was three years ago. I think this could really have a shot now."

When David casually brought up the idea of marriage years before, my reaction uncomfortably resembled some kind of commitment-induced P.T.S.D. Now, though, I could think and talk about marrying David without the sensation of cinder blocks stacked on my chest, crushing air from my lungs.

"After I see him face-to-face," I continued, "if my memories haven't been distorted by time, then I'm all in. Last time he really put himself out there. Even though I loved him, I just couldn't do it. You know, I just wasn't ready to really commit to a marriage and step-children," I explained.

"But now you're ready," Nolan confirmed.

Nolan was right. I was ready. Since patience was never a skill I'd successfully nurtured, as soon as I hung up with Nolan, I called David's phone. While nervously tapping my fingers on the sofa arm, my call rang to voicemail. *Damn*, I thought. Later that evening, I called again but still no answer. I waited fretfully.

*Now all I have to do is make it happen,* I thought. This didn't intimidate me since I was a person used to making things happen for myself. My personal history was packed with instances of accomplishing substantial goals under less-than-desirable circumstances. When obstacle-jumping becomes habit, confidence in your own ability to shape your life solidifies. For me, though, this confidence was not a peaceful one. Behind the self-assurance was a relentless and restless drive prodding me forward until I earned what my heart sought.

The following day, David texted saying he was available if I wanted to talk. Immediately, I called.

He answered his phone, "Well, hello there!"

In response I said with certainty, "I want you to come see me this weekend."

He started laughing then said, "Do you have radar?"

"What do you mean?" I asked.

He explained he was sitting in a hospital bed recovering from the surgery that would give him his sexual function back.

"I can't travel for a few weeks but, yes, I'll come see you."

Nervous yet overjoyed, the days sandwiched between that call and the day of the visit inched by at an infuriating pace. Despite time's slow and stubborn passing, our conversations ramped up. Our daily talks evolved from friendly to flirtatious. But it was a cautious flirtation, in part, because we did not know how it would be coming together after years apart. Would it be uncomfortable? Also, ours was an intensely physical relationship and there was no way to know if it would be like it was before. Even though the surgery made sex possible, would it be awkward or even difficult?

Finally, the day of his visit arrived. When I opened my front door and he turned familiarly, smiling at me, all my concerns evaporated. In place of awkwardness, his gray eyes connected with my blue and the air electrified around us. In a rush, he was in my arms and we were kissing like he'd just returned from war.

Amid ecstatic conversation, light laughter, and endless kissing, our clothes just fell away naturally. Once we were skin against skin, any remaining worries vanished as our bodies took over and he entered me.

By noon the next day, hunger drove us from my bed. In my kitchen just as the scent of coffee clung to the heavy Florida air, we clung to one another. Sweeping his black hair back from his brow, gently I moved my hands to each side of his face.   Tenderly, I guided his face toward mine. My lips brushed his lightly. Feeling the air pulsing around us, I looked into his eyes and said, "David, I am still in love with you."

For the next two heartbeats, I held my breath, only exhaling when a smile lit his face and he kissed me deeply. Then coming up for air, he said,

"I love you too, Sloane. I never stopped loving you."

And there we were again, right where we left off three years before.

David left reluctantly that Sunday with me not wanting him to go. As part of a last effort to tempt him away from the airport, I did not even bother to get dressed before kissing him goodbye. Then, as David walked out the door, loneliness walked in. With 'the fix' I needed to satisfy my reawakened addiction getting further away every moment, I sat on my bed to sulk.

Sulking is dull business, though. Soon I pulled my Tarot card deck out of my nightstand drawer. David was always entertained by my proficiency with the occult. He said it just seemed so out of place with someone who was the most scientific-minded person he knew.  He was right; in science I trusted. I was not even remotely superstitious. Still, I found it fascinating that throughout history people developed Rune Sticks, Astrology to interpret meaning from the constellations, and all kinds of strategies to try to catch a glimpse of what was ahead. Since the beginning of human history, people created these methods to deal with life's uncertainty. Considering humanity's long-standing obsession with the future, I found this unifying factor across time and cultures something worthy of further understanding. With that, I read anything I could that discussed future-divining strategies.

Since my first obsession was learning, the occult couldn't just be a regular hobby. For one, I did not believe in fortune telling of any kind. Even though I did not take the readings seriously, I couldn't just put the Tarot cards or whatever I was using away when I was done then go on with my day. With Tarot, for instance, after each reading, I kept meticulous records with the date I did the reading, the question asked, the cards drawn, and my interpretation of their meanings. In other words, I was collecting data. While I didn't know what I was looking for in particular, I was waiting for the data to accumulate then I would look for patterns.

For this reading, I asked a straightforward question intending to do a simple forecast reading with three cards representing the past, present, and future. I asked: Will I have a future with David?

Turning the first card over, the card representing the past was the Sun. Since the Sun card indicated vitality and happiness, the sun's implications seemed self-evident. This card reminded me of the warm years David and I had while we dated during my time in graduate school.

The middle card represented the present. Once revealed, it showed the Moon. The Moon card, with its mysterious overtones, suggested dreams, not seeing things as they are, uncertainty, and even deception. Particularly following such an amazing weekend, it seemed like a poor fit for the circumstances. I could come up with only one possible interpretation. Perhaps the Moon indicated I was deceiving myself about my readiness for commitment. Feeling quite certain this was not the case, I found my interpretation unsatisfactory. Getting the Moon was not a great omen, though, if one believed in omens.

When I turned over the card representing the future, it showed the Queen of Swords. The Queen's image on the card looked very stern and cold. Often this card represents an intellectual woman. Like most Tarot cards, it has a connection to a specific career path as well. Commonly, the Queen of Swords is associated with writers.

*Okay,* I thought, *that does not tell me anything about my future with David.* My best guess at a suitable interpretation was that possibly it represented me and my tendency to be absorbed in my work and the intellectual world. While I considered myself a writer, to date I'd only published articles and books about my research. While technically qualifying as a published author, more typically I associated the 'writing professions' attached to the Queen of Swords with creative writers, the kind who write stuff people actually enjoy reading. By contrast, I was pretty certain everything I had ever published was only useful for most people when they used it to prop up a table with uneven legs.

# A Family Affair
## Chapter 5

A local British Bistro was hosting a magic-themed high tea event. All week, my twins talked of nothing else. Before entering the café with its tables organized into long rows, the twins insisted David and I go in first to get seated. They wanted to make their dramatic entrance independently.

With each twin opening one of the restaurant's French doors, the bright Florida sun back-lit their costumes, contrasting with the Bistro's interior which was darkly decorated to look like a castle. Both twins wore billowing, black robes hanging open over identical outfits. With black slacks, Avery and Beck each wore a gray V-neck sweater over a white button up shirt punctuated with a well-knotted maroon and gold striped tie. Avery had her strawberry blond bangs swept to the side and her long, light red mane pulled back then tucked under and fastened with bobby pins. This gave the impression of a shorter, more masculine haircut that bore a striking resemblance to Beck's hair.

Soon the 'identical' twins were situated at our table, cloth napkins across their laps.

"Mom, what do you think they will serve for high tea?" asked Avery.

"Well, to be fair, this is my first magical tea of any variety," I said. "So, I'm really not sure."

"So, are you two the same character from a magical story?" David asked.

Avery and Beck exchanged glances with raised eyebrows.

"No, we are the identical wizard twins from Harry Potter," explained Beck.

"We have never heard any magical stories that have two magic fraternal twins," said Avery.

Beck nodded then said, "Yep, it's an unfortunate oversight in the magical story genre."

"Clearly," said David, with a grin.

Having repurposed one of my former graduation robes, I wore a high-collared black shirt showing from underneath the neck opening of my black robe. A pair of wire-rimmed reading glasses were set low on my nose and my red hair was pulled up into a tight bun, just visible under my black, pointed witch hat. Per the twin's request, I'd dressed as a professor of magic.

While David, too, was dressed in another of my graduation gowns and wore a pointed, black hat, there was debate as to which character he was.

"I'm not sure who David should be because I don't think magic professors have boyfriends," said Avery.

"Well, that sounds like a lonely profession," I said.

"When I was a kid, my favorite magic story was about the infamous magician, Merlin. Maybe that's who I am," suggested David.

"How retro!" said Beck.

"Or if you want to go old school, you could be one of the witches from Macbeth," I suggested.

The twins furrowed their brows in unison.

"The professor is referring to Shakespeare," explained David.

"We know," said Beck and Avery.

"It's just David's a little too, well, man-ish to be a Macbeth witch," stated Beck.

"How do you know about the gender of Macbeth's witches?" asked David.

Before either of the twins could answer, the waitstaff, dressed in black, wearing witch hats, and each carrying a teapot, flowed from the kitchen. As they swirled around tables, the wait-witches and wizards poured tea for us and the other guests.

By the end of the magical high tea, I'd made up my mind. I knew I wanted to marry David. There were a few kid-related considerations I needed to make first, though.

When I was a kid myself, my three younger siblings and I would press my mom, trying to get her to say which one of us she liked best. After telling us for probably the one thousandth time that she loved each of us equally, we changed tactics.

"Okay then, do you love us or dad more?"

To us, this seemed like an important question because we knew our parents started dating in high school. Then, despite the likelihood of the youthful relationship failing, my parents stayed together. Even stranger still, they were happy. When I'd see my dad pull my mom from what she was doing in order to sneak a spontaneous kiss, that was just a normal day in our house. Similarly, one evening before bed, I went into my parents' room where my mom, in her nightgown, was fixing her hair and make-up.

"What are you doing? Why are you bothering to put on make-up before going to sleep?" I asked, wondering if my mom was trying to get a jump on the morning or something.

"You'll understand when you are older," she said as she dabbed perfume on her wrists.

And I did understand when I was older. I understood my parents loved each other. I also understood they were screwing like a couple of lions.

Side note: Now, I realize most people say "bunnies" instead of "lions" but that's really misleading. While bunnies have short gestation periods and thus can produce litters quickly, lions and lionesses are the animals whose sexual prowess should be the pinnacle for comparison. That's because when a lioness is in heat, mating bouts can go for days, with pairs of lions bumping uglies up to 40 times per day. See, now that's impressive!

Back to my point. So, my siblings and I asked my mom if she loved us or dad more.

My mom responded, "I love you differently but equally."

Seeing we were not quite satisfied with that response, she explained further, "I will always love all of you, but the main difference is that if dad ever did something really bad to one of you kids, I'd drop him like a hot potato to protect you."

I hadn't expected that response, but I found it surprisingly comforting. With those words, I felt secure in the knowledge that no matter how much my mom loved anyone else in this life - even my dad - that her love for us would come first.

Having always carried that comforting thought with me through the years, this altered how I thought about making a commitment to David. Clearly, I loved David and had loved him for many years. When I felt ready to officially move forward toward a legally-binding commitment, I considered this carefully. In the Fall, before I said anything to David about getting engaged, I bought three rings. (It is all I can do right now not to follow that with, "And one ring to rule them all.")

Shortly thereafter, it was Thanksgiving day. Even though it was just the twins and me, we set the table formally with our nicest china. After we sat down,

I gave each twin a platinum ring each presented in delicate wooden boxes. I explained that the rings were symbols of my love and commitment to them and how my love and commitment to them would always, always come first. Then I explained I was planning on proposing to David.

"When I do propose, I don't want you to think you are being replaced in any way. The three of us are a family and we will always be a family. All we are doing is including David in our circle."

Since my children loved David, this was not a hard sell. What did surprise me, though, was how they seemed genuinely moved by the rings and my proclamation to put them first.

From that moment, my twins and I launched into planning-mode. Since David wasn't available to come see us until after the holidays, we planned every detail for one long January weekend. On the Saturday of David's visit, the twins and I sent David across town to pick up coffee and breakfast for the four of us. While he was out, the twins and I launched into action making a gourmet picnic. We made pasta salad with fresh basil and mozzarella along with tomatoes straight from the garden. We turned chicken breasts, sliced almonds, and purple grapes into what I think of as the Queen Mary of chicken salads. We made a fruit salad with fresh fruit purchased from the Farmer's Market. Pulling a dozen mini apple tarts as well as an equal number of oversized croissants out of the oven, we packed these alongside the various salads neatly into an antique picnic basket. Clearly, this was not a paper plates and Solo cup picnic; it was a fine China, crystal wine glass, and cloth napkin picnic.

With the basket packed, the twins dressed in their new outfits bought especially for the occasion. Since both of them loved retro clothing, my son looked like a young Marlon Brando, with his hat cheekily tilted. My daughter, in her baby blue high-waisted swing dress, reminded me of Judy Garland. My own dress was more present-day, a classic cut in bright red. Since it was made of some sort of over-scienced, man-made fibers, it was impervious to wrinkles and clung to my curves in flattering ways.

When David got back to my house, he carried a large paper bag by its handles and a cardboard tray holding the cups of coffee over to the kitchen table. After David took the bagels and soufflés out of the bag and arranged them in the table's center, we all sat down to eat breakfast together.

Looking around at us in our dressy clothes, David said, "Um, if I knew everyone was going to look so fancy, I would have picked up something nicer for breakfast than Panera."

We assured him Panera was perfect; we were dressed for what we had planned for the afternoon.

Raising his eyebrows, David said, "I take it I need to put on something nicer than jeans then?"

Smiling I said, "Yeah, you might."

Once the carry-on sized picnic basket and other picnic accessories were loaded into my car, David opened my car door for me. Before I stepped in, he wrapped an arm around my waist.

Pulling me in for a kiss he said, "You look like Jessica Rabbit!"

Laughing, I imitated the character's sultry voice, "I'm not bad; I'm just drawn this way."

The drive started on a four-lane interstate. From the interstate, we followed increasingly diminutive roads until eventually we wound our way up a long, gravel lane. Twisting our way to the top of a hill, the lane opened into a parking lot. The parking lot wasn't what you noticed, though. The ordinary gravel lot was overshadowed by an extraordinary Tuscan-style building that housed the winery, set in front of a backdrop of lush green, hilly vineyards.

On the backside of the winery facing the rows of grapevines, the twins set up the picnic at a long wooden, trestle picnic table. This left David and me free to go inside the winery and taste wines until we found one to have with our picnic.

Gathered around a "U" shaped bar in the center of the Winery's spacious shop, we tasted a range of reds and whites. Though Florida is not known for its grape-growing nor wine-making, we tasted several white wines we liked as well as others we didn't.

Our least favorite was one David said, "Oh my! That tastes far too much like that stuff you use to take off your fingernail polish!"

Finally, David and I chose simple bottle of white table wine that was light and mildly buttery. With the newly purchased bottle of chilled bottle wine in-hand, we joined the twins at what was now an artfully arranged, picture-perfect picnic.

Appearing as though this was some final exam for good manners, the twins politely offered and passed dishes around to each person. Then the twins advised us of the drink selections and filled our glasses. Breaking for a moment from their role as elegant 1940s movie stars appearing in a picnic scene, they asked me to take a picture of them in their new outfits. My daughter, Avery, reciprocated by taking a picture of David and me. Then joining us back at the table, she spread her linen napkin delicately across her lap.

As lighthearted conversation carried us through lunch, it occurred to me I had no idea what I was going to say when I gave David the ring. *Was I going to get down on one knee? No,* I thought, *not in a dress that cost the equivalent of a mortgage payment. Do I just toss him the little box and say, "Here you go?" Oh my God,* I thought, *I've never been taught how to propose.*

After lunch was finished but before dessert was served, I still hadn't thought of a proposal that seemed suitable for the moment. Out of time and realizing the best I could do at this point was punt, I sat a small package, elegantly wrapped in copper and silver paper in front of David.

"I got you a gift," I said.

David looked surprised and then carefully unwrapped the little package. Inside was a small, walnut box inlaid with Cherry wood. He opened the hinged lid of the wooden box. Within the box, nestled deeply in a white satin cushion, was a white gold engagement band.

David gasped, "This isn't...?"

"Yes, it is!" spouted Beck.

"Mom wants you to marry us," said Avery with poise.

"Oh my God! This is amazing!" he said putting on the ring. "It even fits perfectly."

"Oh my God," he said again as he pulled me into a tight hug and kissed me. "You never cease to surprise me."

"It's one of my talents," I said.

"Let me take your picture!" said my son.

With me standing now, David stood behind me, wrapping his arms around my waist. We smiled for the first picture. As Beck kept snapping shots, David dramatically dipped me as though we were dancing in a romantic movie, then kissing me deeply during the next pictures.

After the impromptu photo shoot, Avery filled up each of our glasses, David and my glasses were topped with white wine, and she and her brother's with Orange Crush. Then Beck raised his glass with his pinky held out as a clear sign he knew how to handle such a refined moment. In response, we each raised our own glasses.

After a dramatic pause, Beck said "Mawwiage is what bwings us together today."

After quoting the movie, *Princess Bride*, to good effect, my son finished with "Cheers!"

Above the picnic still spread across the table, we clinked our glasses to mark our excitement for the beautiful day and for all the beautiful tomorrows ahead as part of our circle, now bigger by one.

# Magic and Medicine
## Chapter 6

A pine tree wouldn't work well because the branches are too far from the ground," said David.

"Nothing with flowers—I hate bees," said Beck, now 13 years old.

"Then nothing with fruit, either," said Avery. David and Beck nodded.

"Live Oaks have really thick branches so that'd be good," said David.

As I walked into the room, my son said, "Mom, we have decided. We want a Live Oak Tree."

"Um, David, am I supposed to know what Beck's talking about?" I asked.

"It's their 'must have'—you asked us to let you know what our 'must haves' are for the new house," explained David.

"See," said Beck, "David, Avery, and I are going to build a treehouse and we need the right kind of tree. So, the main thing I care about in whatever new house we pick is it has to have a big tree with fat branches, preferably a Live Oak, so we can build the tree house."

Avery held up a large piece of drawing paper showing various sketches of treehouses. One of the drawings showed a front view of a treehouse with a large window opening.

"What do you think?" asked Avery.

"Love them!" I said of the sketches. "Since it is so hot in Florida, I'd suggest putting that big rectangular window on both the front wall and the back wall. That way a breeze will blow through and it won't get so hot inside the treehouse."

"Oooo, good idea, mom," said Beck. "Also, I want to get some battery-powered fans like the ones our neighbor has in their garage." Then pointing at the sketch with his pencil, Beck said, "And here, instead of an open doorway, I think we need some kind of gate or something. Mom, I don't want you to come up into the treehouse to visit then accidentally fall out," said Beck.

"Hey, I'm not *that* clumsy," I said with a grin.

"Didn't you fall out of that little Crape Myrtle tree when you were trimming branches?" asked Avery.

"Well okay, there was that *one* time," I said.

"Mom, how many trees have you tried to climb since we were born?" asked Beck.

"One," I said sheepishly.

"Avery, correct me if I'm wrong, but I'm pretty sure that means mom has fallen out of 100% of the trees she's climbed in the last 1 ½ decades," said Beck.

"That is correct," said Avery, with a nod.

"I was thinking we'd make the treehouse doorway extra wide so we could attach a cargo net to use as a ladder," suggested David. "If we mount it on a slant like this," said David holding his hand at a 45-degree angle, "then it will be easier to climb as well as having the added advantage of breaking your mom's fall should she tumble out of the doorway."

Avery and Beck snickered. Holding up his hand to temper the laughter, David said with mock seriousness, "I'm not saying you're clumsy, Sloane. Really it's safer for everyone." Then David winked toward Avery and Beck.

"Mom, don't you always say, 'Tending to the safety and welfare of the occupants is the first rule in building design?'" asked Beck.

"Well, yes," I said.

"See, we are just making good design choices just in case anyone," then pausing to jerk her head in my direction, "might find themselves plummeting towards the ground," said Avery.

"So, a big tree is your only must-have?" I asked the twins.

"No," said Avery and Beck in unison.

"We also need our own bathrooms," explained Avery.

"We are too old to share," added Beck.

"Plus, it takes Beck like 30 minutes to do his hair."

"Hey, the effortless look takes time."

"What about you David?" I asked.

"I'm easy. I just want enough space to store my tools and maybe a workshop area."

"Do you want a separate bedroom for each of your boys?"

"Nah, since my oldest, Mark, is grown, he probably won't be here much. I think Chris will mostly be here over summers, so one room should be more than enough for the boys."

Since Chris was older than the twins, David explained Chris wanted to finish high school up North and planned to visit us during vacations.

"Well, all that seems easy enough. Now all we have to do is find an ugly, old house that needs a complete remodel, then I'll work my magic."

After a couple false starts in finding a house—one we rejected because it was on a flood plain and another house because we were outbid, finally we chose a house 'with good bones' that was in a great location. Since David wouldn't be selling his house until he moved to Florida the following summer, I sold my house to buy the one we planned to remodel.

With David still living out of state and I being so busy at work, I decided to hire a contractor rather than doing the contracting myself. When David and I interviewed several potential contractors, we did not find any particularly impressive. Consequently, we settled on the one we found least distasteful, the best of a bad lot.

Since the plans I'd drawn for the remodel required the house's interior to be completely gutted as well as changing some of the openings for doors and windows in the exterior wall, the upcoming project was the most extensive I'd ever designed. Despite the magnitude of the project, the contractor was confident that he could get a portion of the house remodeled so the twins and I could move in within six weeks following demolition.

Familiar with the dubiousness of contractor deadlines, I signed a three-month lease on an apartment. When there were just two weeks left on my lease, I discussed the project's slow progress with the contractor. Since he was certain the house would be livable before my lease was up, I signed a non-renewal agreement with the apartment complex. The day before my lease ended, the contractor called to say he was not going to be able to meet the deadline.

"How much longer?" I asked.

"A week. Two at most," the contractor promised.

So, with a pick-up truck rented from Home Depot, the twins and I stacked boxes and furniture into its bed then moved everything from the apartment into a storage unit. Afterwards, my two teenagers, our dog Meatloaf, and I moved into a single hotel room.

In the hotel, Avery hated the close quarters and complained incessantly. The only one of us who hated it more was Meatloaf. Outwardly it was a nice hotel with crown moldings and a stone fireplace in the lobby. Even so, how it functioned was a different matter entirely.

From inside our room, we could hear doors closing, chairs shuffled across the wood floors, and the numerous conversations taking place in surrounding rooms and adjacent levels of the hotel. As a result, Meatloaf seemed to think we were being invaded. While normally not a dog to bark much, Meatloaf was constantly alerting us whenever he heard any one of the almost-constant nearby noises.

While we found Meatloaf's panicked barking a reason to sympathize with his confusion about the implications of the hotel's poor acoustics, the guests in neighboring rooms were less understanding about his constant racket. This meant our rotating slate of neighbors hated us, each in turn. Day and night, we received obligatory calls from the manager who was required to let us to know when there had been a complaint. Even Meatloaf, looking like the caramel-colored offspring of an Ewok who mated with Fozzie Bear, wasn't enough to earn forgiveness from the neighbors.

Several nights when neighbors were up late and making noise, Meatloaf was on guard, barking even at the sound of every chair moved on the imitation wood floor and every door closing. To avoid drawing the wrath of our neighbors, I took Meatloaf out to the car with me. I hoped that with fewer distractions, we might be able to get some sleep.

After leaning both front seats back as far as they would go, I sat Meatloaf on the passenger's seat, and I got in on the driver's side. As I rolled up a sweatshirt to use as a pillow, Meatloaf climbed over the center console that separated the two front seats. Having surmounted that obstacle, he promptly climbed onto my lap. With a sigh, I returned Meatloaf to his own seat. Despite my explanation detailing how we would both sleep well if we had our own spaces, he stood there, staring back at me with big, sad, brown eyes.

"I really need to sleep, Meatloaf," I explained again. "You rest over there."

Seeming like he understood, I rested my head on my sweatshirt and closed my eyes. Following some clicks of his nails on the center console, Meatloaf climbed back onto my lap.

Digging around in the backseat, I found one of the twin's sweatshirts. Folding the sweatshirt, I made a make-shift doggie mattress to cover the center console unit with its cup holders. Offering the upgraded center console to Meatloaf, he reluctantly accepted the compromise and settled in.

A full five months after demolition, the twins, Meatloaf, and I moved into a very dusty and still very much under-construction house. When David visited, we worked together on parts of the house's renovation. Since he was doing the wiring, sometimes I helped as his assistant, fastening on outlet covers or pulling wire. Other times, I hung towel bars or did other small jobs. I was much better at creating the house's design in drafting software than actually building it, but still David and I enjoyed working together.

After we mentioned precisely that—how much we liked working together— several different times, we started discussing the idea of starting a remodeling business together. Our thought was I would be involved part-time, but it could be David's full-time work when he moved to Florida.

Excited about the possible new venture, I began researching potential business names as well as designing a logo for the business. When David was back in the Midwest between visits, I'd email revisions of the logo to him for feedback. Having a future of possibilities open before us made everything seem light and fresh. For a time, we even forgot about David's cancer that hadn't completely resolved but was not progressing either.

After a year of construction that also marked 1 ½ years of engagement, finally David and I found ourselves hanging pictures and putting the finishing touches on what would soon be *our* house. The house, with its freshly painted walls, white stone see-thru fireplace, and rich walnut floors was starting to match the life I'd imagined living with David.

Since it was the week of the twins' birthday and in order to complete the final details on the house, David visited for eight days. With one of his sons in college and the other son dual-enrolling in college during his upcoming senior year of high school, the next time David came to Florida he would be staying permanently.

"Just think, the next time you're here you won't be a visitor," I said as David hung a picture on the wall. With the picture hung, he bent down to put the hammer back in the toolbox. As he stood up again, he winced and rubbed his back.

"Are you okay?" I asked.

"Just a little achy. I'm not as young as I used to be."

Beyond the birthday celebration, David took full advantage of this time to spoil us with elegant dinners out and surprise trips to a local ice cream parlor. Collectively, everyone's spirits reflected the joy and laughter of our time together.

On a morning mid-week, I eyed David from the other room as he shook some tablets into his hand and tossed them into his mouth. Once he returned the bottle to his pocket, he began shaking coffee grounds into the coffee maker. With the intention of asking about all the pills, I walked up behind David and wrapped my arms around his waist.

Just as he closed the lid on the coffee maker, Beck walked into the kitchen in mid-verse, singing/rapping a song from the musical, "Hamilton." David, whose love of live theater and musicals was very familiar to us, joined in on the song.

After dramatically completing a couple verses, David and Beck took small bows.

Avery, who'd been drawn to kitchen during the performance, applauded loudly along with me.

Then I kissed David on the cheek and said, "I just love how perfectly you fit right into our lives."

"I love you, Sloane," David said, smiling in response.

With only two days until David headed back to Wisconsin, I was still at the height of the buzz that came with such a happy week. After the twins went to friends' houses for the night, David took the opportunity during this private moment to share some news.

Suddenly serious, David said, "Sloane, I went to the oncologist recently and it didn't go well."

He explained that despite the cancer being stalled for several years, this was no longer the case. It had metastasized and spread drastically.

"How bad is it?" I asked.

"It's everywhere."

"What will they do then?"

"They said there aren't any more options to try. My doctor said to get my affairs in order."

I gasped. Then through the lump now choking my throat, I asked, "How long do you have?"

"A month, maybe two, with increasing weakness and pain."

"No! We are finally getting…" then a sob rose from my chest.

David's eyes filled with tears. "It sucks."

"No, this can't…" then I put my face into my hands and wept.

Tears rolled freely down David's face. As he wrapped his arms around me, he said "I'm so sorry."

"Don't."

"I just hate this."

Hours later and exhausted from crying, he took my hand, guiding me toward my room. When he pulled me past the bed, curiosity paused my tears. He didn't stop until we were next to my sleek, modern shower. Since neither of us had turned on the light, the bathroom's clerestory windows washed us in an ocean-colored glow.

Since the shower was so spacious as to not need a door, David paused, kissed away the two tears still clinging to my cheeks, then leaned inside to turn on the water.

As the temperature of the water rose, David slipped the thin straps of my red nightgown from my shoulders, watching me as the satiny fabric slid to the floor. The shower's steam licked at my bare skin. As David paused to pull his shirt over his head, I unbuttoned his jeans, pushing them from his hips.

Once all our clothes were pooled on the bathroom floor, he drew me into the shower and under the rush of hot water. With my back to the water it rained down, drenching my red mane. Following the water's lead, he smoothed his hands along the length of my hair.

I poured body wash into my hands then ran them down the length of his broad chest, leaving a bubbling wake of suds behind. David removed his hands from my hair that now clung to my shoulders and upper back. His fingertips traced my back then butt. Pausing, he lifted me up. As I wrapped my legs around him tightly, he pierced me deeply.

We drenched each other in a flood of touch and steamy kisses as the water washed over us. David turned us, pushing my back up against the white tiled shower wall. Then pushed into me, hard.

I gasped from the pleasure of it, but I was not able to move in the way I wanted so I said, "Bed. Now," then I reached over and shut off the water.

Still inside me, David carried me into the bedroom, pouring me on top of the comforter.

"I love you," whispered David, as he pushed deeply into me.

I kissed him hard instead of answering with words. Frenzied, I tried to memorize every movement, every glance, but the harder I tried, the more quickly each evaporated.

When David headed back north to his home again, for the last time, even my bones ached. During the past couple years while David and I were together but living apart, geography seemed irrelevant because David always felt like my home. As he left to catch a plane that morning, I longed to leave with him but with classes still in session at the University I couldn't just leave for some indefinite period. Instead I kissed him goodbye, looking into his sad eyes, and felt the future we'd hoped for ripped away as he walked out of the door. Suddenly, I'd become some world-weary refugee who had lost her home.

Without the energy to do life, I went back to bed. For two days, I stayed in my pajamas, rarely leaving my bedroom. Soon, doing nothing became unbearable. There had to be something I could do. But what? The doctors couldn't even help David. With creaks and groans, the wheels in my head began to move joltingly.

Sitting up in bed, I pulled my laptop from my nightstand. Opening the computer, I stared at the screen as it flashed to life. *I have a problem that needs to be solved.* Researchers always start with a question. My question: *what treatment alternatives exist that wouldn't fall into David's oncologist's training?* Then I went into full-blown research mode.

In my frantic search, I read research articles about experimental treatments and alternative medicines. I read about acupuncture and even folk remedies. I read people's personal accounts in trying various options. Then I came across one thing that sounded like it might be useful.

The backstory was that a mid-twentieth-century nurse successfully used an herbal mixture which originally came from an American Indian medicine man. To create this cancer treatment, the nurse grew her own herbs from which she concocted a medicinal tea. According to online records, it was important the herbs used in the tea were fresh from the garden in order to be the proper potency.

Perhaps even more remarkable than the possible existence of a cancer-treating tea was the fact this nurse held firm for decades to the conviction that the treatment only be used to help people and not for profit-making. In her clinic, she treated patients who were told by their doctors there was no further help nor hope. Despite the odds, her clinical records showed a surprising amount of success. With those successes to her credit, companies and governments eventually tried buying the potentially profitable formula from her, still she would not sell it.

By that point, I liked this stubborn nurse and her ideals. While there was very little research on her formula, I was able to read some of the nurse's original notes a contemporary relative of hers apparently had uploaded to the web. By then I was determined David should try this herbal treatment. Since there wasn't time for checking and re-checking my sources, I ordered the herbs immediately.

Already dried and prepared to be made into tea, I had these delivered to David along with a mug that read, "You're awesome. Keep that shit up!" Upon receiving these, David promised me he would keep making the medicinal tea and drinking the doses I recommended until "the end."

Since the twentieth century nurse's notes indicated the herbs worked best fresh, I also placed orders for the various herb seeds, which I planted in neat rows within a new section of my garden. I hoped the prepared herbs I sent to David could keep him alive until the fresh herbs grew. Then I planned to brew the medicinal tea for him myself.

Once every weed was pulled from the garden and every seed tucked into an inch rich soil then carefully watered, I found myself literally waiting on plants to grow. Needing to busy myself with something - anything - that might be useful, the only thing I could think to do was a Tarot reading to ask if this herbal treatment would work.

While there are many ways to do a reading, like a more complicated ten card Celtic Cross, I kept it simple by doing a Past, Present, Future reading. After asking my question aloud, I dealt three cards face-down. Turning over the first card representing the past, it showed eight straight wooden staffs at a slight angle. This, the Eight of Wands, symbolized swift action and expansion. Also, it represented self-reliance and things changing quickly. *This*, I thought, *seemed appropriate considering I'd just rushed to read so much research to help David if I could.*

The present card was the Seven of Swords. Often this card indicated hidden plans as well as trying to get away with something secretly. Further, this card implied that concealed plan would go awry, ultimately revealing the secret. In the context of David's illness, did this refer to the herbal formula and its usefulness being kept from the general public? If so, then I reasoned the revelation could be me finding information about this treatment regardless of attempts to keep it unknown.

Once turned, the future card showed the Nine of Cups. This card represented contentment and enjoying life. Also, it signified time for harvesting what is sown. Regarding the whole suit of Cups, this suit was a water sign, which broadly represented emotions. Did this card suggest that the herbs would help? Was harvesting what was sown literal here? Did it mean the herbs, once freshly harvested, would be the cure we were looking for, and thus be the key to us living out our lives happily together? As was my habit I took out my hardbound graph paper notebook and wrote down the information about this Tarot reading. After I recorded the details, I closed the hard, black cover with a sigh. This time, for the first time, I really hoped the Universe, through the Tarot cards, was letting me peek at the coming future.

# Blank Pages

## Chapter 7

knew from past experience, space was what David needed in tough times. With that, I tried to be patient with the fact my job was holding me hostage in Florida and even if it hadn't been, David still wanted to be alone.

Even so, I pressed, "David, I can't stand this. Please let me just come and be there with you. Are the boys doing the cooking and keeping the house in order?"

"We are fine, babe," said David. "Plus, you know you can't leave your kids and your job.'"

I didn't answer.

"If I feel up to it, Mark is going to drive us up to the cabin this weekend. You know how I love that place."

And I did know, but still I sat silently.

"I just want to sit by the pond and enjoy it..."

The unspoken words, "while I can" weighted the pause that followed.

Then I said, "In a week and a half, we have a Monday off and the kids will be with their dad."

"Sloane…"

"Before you say 'no' please just consider the possibility of me coming up for a day or two. Please. Just think about it."

Silence.

"And what am I going to do if things change quickly while I'm stuck here? How will I even know what's going on?" I asked.

After a moment's thought, he said, "I will have Mark promise to contact you if I, if I can't call you myself."

At his remote cabin in the northern Wisconsin woods, David didn't have a cell signal, leaving me impatient to hear his voice. He and Mark expected to be back home by Sunday night, or perhaps Monday at the latest.

Then Sunday came and went. Once it was Monday morning, I was worried but knew it was still too early to panic. That evening, with the kids at their dad's, I came home from work to an empty house except for the ever-excited Meatloaf, anxiously awaiting my arrival. Once inside, I paused to pat his downy head before heading into my room to get showered and changed.

With my damp skin wrapped in an oversized bathrobe and pressing my wet hair with a towel, I came back into the family room, refreshed. I sat down on the sofa next to Meatloaf who had fallen asleep beside my phone. I picked up the phone and the screen sprang to life. Hoping to see a message or a missed call from David, suddenly I sat up straighter when instead I saw I had a message from Mark's phone. *No! This couldn't...*I thought. *It hadn't even been a month yet. Only a couple weeks had passed since David was here, in this room. For a long moment,* I stared at the locked screen before touching my phone's home button with my thumb.

Clinging to the phone like my life depended upon it, I read the text. The message told me they'd come home the night before because David wasn't well then, he lost his dad in the middle of the night.

Tears rained freely down my cheeks. "I thought he had more time," I typed.

"Actually, he was with us longer than the doctor said. I know he didn't want you to worry."

I gasped, then sobbed harder.

*I should've just gone. To hell with my job.*

Feeling a bit dizzy, I typed, "When is the funeral?"

"Well, dad wanted to be cremated and he made us promise we wouldn't waste money on a funeral," he wrote.

Practical as ever, that sounded very much like the David I knew.

"Your dad was the best man I've ever known," I wrote.

"I hope I can be just half the man he was," Mark responded.

"He saw a lot of himself in you. I have no doubt you will make him proud."

"I hope so. I know he loved you very much," said Mark.

"And I him. Even though you and your brother have lots of family up there, please don't hesitate to ask is there is anything I can do for you."

Of the weeks that followed, I remembered very little, or perhaps I chose not to remember that time. As it stood, those weeks were like blank pages in my head—with each page accounting for the passage of time, but these long swaths of time were linked with only vague splashes of content.

Like a dark inkblot on a pristine page, I did remember seeing my teenaged twins visibly aching from the loss of their step-father-to-be. Instinctually, mothers just want to do what mothers do—fix what is broken. Since death isn't fixable, I was more spectator than mother.

Beck, who was particularly crazy about David, said little but the heavy weight of his grief was obvious. Instead of bounding in the front door and raiding the refrigerator for pizza rolls, mozzarella sticks, ice cream sandwiches or sometimes all the above, Beck came home and just sat on the sofa. Since Meatloaf saw this as an invitation to cuddle, he ran in an excited circle, then hopped up next to Beck, nudging Beck's hand with his cold nose. Instead of engaging, Beck stood up, patted Meatloaf on the head and said, "I don't feel like playing now," then retreated to his room until I called him for dinner.

After Beck pushed the food around on his dinner plate for the fifth night in a row instead of eating, I told Beck I thought it might help if he talked to someone.

Expecting a flat refusal, I was shocked when Beck just nodded his head, stood up and said, "I'm going to go do homework."

While Beck's grief appeared to be directed inward, Avery's was the opposite. She'd write poems about missing David or draw pictures of us all together. In truth, I did not want to hear the poems when Avery asked to read them aloud. I knew hearing the potent, raw pain of my daughter would lance my own wounds. Not ready for all my wounds to be laid open, I let Avery read them while I pretended to listen intently. To drown out her words, inside my head I silently recited song lyrics or poems I had memorized when I was a young.

Afterwards, I'd say, "Your writing is beautiful, Avery. I'm sure David would be really touched."

Then Avery would lean in for a hug before running off to use her grief as further fuel to drive her creativity.

Just weeks after David's death, Beck was meeting twice a week with a therapist who specialized in grief counseling. A couple weeks after that the therapist had Beck also seeing the pediatric psychiatrist in his practice. After the psychiatrist met with Beck, he called me into his office and sent Beck out in order to explain to me Beck's state as he viewed it.

"Beck said it was okay if I shared a few things with you. He seems to be blaming himself in some way for David's death," said the doctor.

"Well, that doesn't make any sense. David died from cancer."

"Yes, and Beck knows that, but he feels very guilty because when you and David got back together a couple years ago, he said he felt like he was never as close to David as he used to be. And somehow, Beck worried that he did something wrong and failed David in some way."

With my mouth agape, I nodded.

"I am concerned that if we do not intervene there is a possibility Beck might hurt himself."

"Why?" I gasped.

"These things are complicated. Does depression run in your or Beck's father's family?"

"Yes," I said, "It does."

The doctor nodded as though I'd confirmed his suspicion.

"Well, I want to start him on this," he said, handing me a paper prescription. "When I asked, Beck said he was willing to try medication."

I nodded, then the doctor continued, "With everything considered, I'd like to see Beck again soon, to make sure the medication is helping and to monitor the dosage."

Wordless, I nodded again. "He's going to be okay?" I asked, looking for reassurance.

"Just keep an eye on him and try to keep him from isolating himself," he said in place of words of comfort.

Then he handed me a crisp brochure, which I accepted blindly, then I mumbled, "Thanks," as I left the office.

Even at the best moments, it is a struggle to keep a teenager from holing up in his/her room. So, I kept trying to think of excuses to do things together such as baking cookies or watching movies. The more I tried, the more this seemed to irritate Beck.

Although not typically a snappy teen, when I made any suggestion, he'd gripe, "I'm too busy," or "You're disturbing me."

Instead of immediately reacting to his abrupt retorts, I waited. Then one evening I found a calm tone and said, "Beck it seems like you have been more easily aggravated than usual lately."

With the patented teenager eye roll, Beck parried with, "No, mom. You've just been more annoying than usual," then he retreated to his room.

Several weeks after starting the medication, I was running low on new ways to keep Beck from sulking alone.

Lacking any better ideas, I said, "Hey Beck, let's go shoot some baskets."

Beck's eyes widened and a singular laugh escaped his lips, "Seriously, mom?"

"Yes, seriously!" I said, conjuring bravado.

"But, mom, your ol…"

Putting my hand on my hips, I squinted my eyes and huffed at him.

"I mean, you are youth-challenged and I'm like a foot taller than you."

"Are you scared that your lil' mommy might beat you?" I pretended a whine, pulling my lip into a pout.

"You are on, small one!" Beck exclaimed, jumping to his feet.

And so, it was after weeks of therapy, medication, and a game of basketball, the turning point came for Beck.

With me breathing overly hard and sweat pasting my hair to my head, we headed back into the house after our game.

Without displaying the smallest sign of exertion, Beck grinned, "Don't feel bad, Mom. You put up a good fight out there."

"Feel bad? I don't feel bad! I was awesome!"

"I felt like I was playing an asthmatic second grader!"

"Well, this asthmatic second grader stole the ball from you! Twice!"

Beck smiled his beautiful, toothy smile, the one I hadn't seen in far too long, then said, "What was I thinking? You were a superstar!"

Patting my head, he added, "What's for dinner, little one? Kicking your butt in basketball made me hungry."

# British Invasion

## Chapter 8

Before the sun was up this morning, I wrote a check for my kids' field trip. With that, I noticed the date was exactly three months since David's death. Cloudy and wretched, I'd struggled but managed to keep afloat in my own pain.

Through those weeks, friends made suggestions to help me heal.

The most common thought whispered in unison with a sympathetic head tilt was, "Sloane, you are going through so much. You need to keep a journal to work through your feelings."

At first, I didn't take their suggestions, at least not until one day when B.S. was in charge of my brain, leaving me in a hazy spiral of unproductive panic in my office. Rather than be consumed by it, in the oppressive heat of the late afternoon sun, I walked to the University Bookstore. Inside the Union Building, I stood waiting in the bookstore check-out line. In one hand I held a new journal to purchase and in the other, I held my library card rather than the credit card I intended. As buying the journal was my big accomplishment for the day, I felt I owed it to myself to get up early to write in it. With the field trip check written, I opened the new journal and wrote.

*Monday, Sept. 4ᵗʰ, 6:45 A.M.*

*Last night I was sitting on my bed all Clark Kent-headed having a good laugh about B.S. trying to buy this journal with my library card. For the first time since David died, I felt a few seconds of peace. Just as I recognized it as a peaceful moment, I froze. That's because I remembered there's some cosmic idiosyncrasy triggered when life calms, even for a short time. As soon as you stop paying attention to life and start to coast, the Universe reminds you she likes to be the center of attention; and based on my experience, the Universe can be a real bitch. Since she was already trouncing me, I hoped I might get a pass this time. Perhaps I might get a pass, if I was normal, but I'm not normal. I'm a beacon for The Absurd.*

If, like me, you know you are destined for whatever life outcome will most amuse onlookers, still this comes with an upside. For instance, in my late twenties, a suspicious symptom occurred suddenly. With my young children past breastfeeding age and knowing for certain I was not pregnant, I suddenly started lactating, but only from one breast. When I reported this oddity to my doctor, she ordered a scan to check for a brain tumor. Since past experience consistently showed The Absurd always trumped every other possible option, this meant whatever trial or tragedy this symptom indicated would turn out to be something far too embarrassing to elicit pity, as a brain tumor was likely to do. My destiny's warped path bypassed sad calamities like broken vertebrae or cancers.

While this comedic twist on tragedy protected me from some ailments, it greatly increased the likelihood of others. For example, one winter when I was a kid, my dad set my brother and I up like dominos on our red, plastic sled. After a big push, we sped down the icy hill. To my annoyance, my brother's knit cap-covered head blocked my view, hampering my excitement. To fix said problem, I just leaned far to one side then…

*WHAM!*

Out of nowhere a towering pine tree leapt into my way and, with a sickening crack, smacked me in the face with its trunk. Knocking me off the sled, I lay in the snow wailing, my mitten-covered hands shielding my throbbing nose and face.

Until then, the only kids I knew with broken appendages came to school the next day with a hard but gleaming white cast and a pocket full of Sharpie markers. Then at recess, we took turns writing and drawing small pictures on the fresh, rough surface.

Sitting in the doctor's office after the sledding accident with a clearly broken nose, I asked, "When are you going to put a cast on it."

With raised eyebrows, the doctor said, "Oh no, you don't need a cast."

My nose ached, felt twice its normal size, and the only thing swelling more quickly than my face was my indignation. Now, I didn't know what they taught at *his* medical school, but my elementary school-aged self was certain when a full-grown pine tree breaks your nose, that accident was cast-worthy. After I explained this - something I viewed as a basic medical principle to the droll and patently unamused doctor - he still said no cast.

"But my nose is broken, right?" I pressed.

"Yes."

"Can't you just wrap the wet cast bandages around my head like a mummy?" Still the doctor said, "No."

As an alternative, I suggested he put a cast on my arm or my leg. Despite my creative problem solving, the doctor said that wouldn't help my nose heal. Clearly, he didn't understand the situation.

Coming to his rescue, in a tone more panicked than intended, I clarified further, "But they just can't go writing on my swollen face with Sharpies because that stuff will never come off!"

The doctor blinked at me. Then, my mom took me home without a cast.

With this long farce serving as my personal history, I never craved excitement. I disliked surprises. When something happened, I wanted that something to be familiar so I could flip through my head's internal index, locating proper instructions for how to best handle the given situation. Even so, the Universe's ideas about the workings of my life differed.

Since that's the case, the Universe never missed opportunities to suitably afflict me with ailments and injuries that even embarrassed my doctors. Included in that long list of humiliating medical situations were an emergency room-worthy case of constipation as well as a predisposition for getting rampant poison ivy, the worst case of which was on my hoo-ha. Even while living with the subtle anxiety of knowing I was a prime candidate for being run over by a parade's length of mini-Shriner cars or perhaps dying from hypothermia after eating too much ice cream, this was my fate and I accepted it.

Consequently, when that doctor suggested the possibility of a brain tumor, it was all I could do to keep from looking at her and saying with a huff, "Fine. I will go in for your...'*scan*'," putting air quotes around scan.

Managing just that once to keep a thought to myself, I went ahead and had the "scan". Sure enough, no brain tumor. Apparently, it is possible to spontaneously lactate from one breast for no detectable reason whatsoever. *Yep, that sounded about right.*

Considering my status as a self-diagnosed lightning rod for chaos, perhaps you can understand why I got a little skittish that morning after first writing in my journal. That is because my ex-husband, Tom, called saying he needed to talk to me later that day. When your ex wants to tell you "something," I imagine it is much the same feeling as being invited to a holiday party at Satan's house. Even if the host gives you a gift, you just know that son-of-a-bitch is going to burn.

When later came, I sat across a small, cafe table from Tom. With his first words, the thunder started rolling.

"My wife and I were trying to send flowers to David's sons, but we couldn't find any information online about where to send them," he said.

"Well, he was cremated. Also, he asked his sons not to waste money on a funeral," I said.

"Still, there should have been something, an obituary, or some bit of information." *Why were he and his wife always such busy-bodies!* I thought.

Besides, I didn't see what the big deal was about not finding an obituary online, but the look on Tom's face told me regardless of whether I saw it or not, it *was* a big deal. Even so, I couldn't think of a response to the unfound obituary so I just sat still, hoping if I didn't make any sudden movements, I wouldn't draw the lightning I felt charging in the air.

"Why do you even care?" I pressed.

Tom frowned, ignored the question and talked on using words like "suspicious", "lawyer", and "checking." Tom was notorious for keeping his lawyer on Speed Dial and for contacting him over anything even loosely related to the law.

The pounding in my ears grew louder and faster, "I don't know what you are getting at," I said with defiance.

"My lawyer found records showing David remarried his ex-wife about three years ago."

Since David and I had been dating this second time for the past 2 ½ years, I stuttered and gaped, unable to make words.

Since I'd visibly lost the ability to speak, Tom continued, "Also, he found no evidence of David's death."

Finding my voice at last, I said, "What? So, you need me to produce a body or something for you?"

As heads turned at nearby tables, I realized I'd spoken louder than I intended.

For a moment, my ex just stared at me. Vaguely I noted my sarcasm was not the life preserver I was hoping it would be.

As my ex-husband outlined each of the "facts" he believed true, my mind short-circuited. I couldn't think at all. When the temporary power came back up, there was only a frantic, blinking red message light reading, "Lies! Lies! Lies!"

Getting seismic news is never pleasant. Even so, when your ex-spouse is the one who gives it to you, this is a level of hell not even Dante imagined. While Tom was gifted at maintaining a steady voice, his mouth, fixed in a self-satisfied sneer, belied his feelings. I wish I could say I maintained a sense of decorum, but dignity was nowhere to be found. Without an anchor like natural grace, fight or flight instinct kicked in and I leapt from my chair. Even sensing many sets of eyes staring at me, I opened my mouth to speak, to shout, but instead of words, a loud sob escaped. Desperate in my humiliation, then I yelled words, lots of them. I can't remember what exactly, but I know I used the expressions "sadistic ass-hat" and "insane manure."

In between my insults and denials, Tom finished explaining. Somewhere in there I heard the words "Facebook" and "wedding pictures." While I knew all these words' meanings, I couldn't make sense of them in this context. David was dependable and faithful. He was kind and selfless. He was a nurturer and always thoughtful. These pieces wouldn't fit together with what my ex was calling "facts." Even when I tried to force the pieces together in my mind, they still wouldn't fit. That's when I really lost it. I was so out of my head, at one point I went British,

"Bloody hell, man! Have you gone mad?!"

I answered my own question, "You have. Of course, that's what it is. This is madness! You must be mad. Doubtless. You have gone bloody mad!"

Then, my British phrase book in my head ran out but still I rambled like an un-medicated mental patient, "That doesn't make any sense. You aren't making any sense. You just don't know. I lost my partner. You don't know anything. Nothing. No. Thing. No. No. NO!"

My ex sat quiet and still, obviously trying not to agitate the crazy lady further. Frantically looking from side-to-side and seeing nothing but wide eyes and gaping mouths, again I lost the ability to form words. After grabbing my purse from the floor beside my chair, I bolted towards the door.

Pausing only long enough to turn and screech, "Mad!" one more time, I stormed off into a rain-drenched parking lot.

I must have driven because I found myself at my own front doors. Suddenly, I couldn't make my hands nor fingers work. I dropped my phone. I picked it up. I dropped a pen. I picked it up. Then I spilled my purse. As I scraped coins, receipts, stray credit cards, and containers of lip balm into an increasingly soggy pile, a baby lizard ran across my hand.

"PISS OFF!" I cursed at the brown, branchy-toed creature as I shoveled a few stray leaves and small sticks into my bag along with my belongings.

After I recalled how locks and keys worked, I sat on the grey leather sofa in my family room. Wildly, I searched the internet. Since B.S. was in charge of my mind, I ran Google search after Google search but found only a small bit of incriminating but uncertain evidence. Stalking my dead-fiancé's ex-wife's Facebook page, I found pictures—clearly taken in recent years—that appeared wedding-ish. *Were they in a play?* I thought wildly. *Sometimes David did Community Theater so, yes, that was possible. It was just a role. David couldn't stand his ex-wife. These must be pictures of a play.*

*What if it wasn't a play, though?* asked a far-away voice in my head. *If it wasn't a play and he married her, it was probably for some practical reason then, like for health insurance. That could be. Even with insurance, cancer treatment in the U.S. is extraordinarily expensive. David and his possibly-current wife likely lived separate lives, having gotten re- married for health coverage.* Still, it seemed unlikely people who married for medical insurance would dress up in wedding clothes and have professional pictures taken. Okay, yes, admittedly that was a snag in my theory.

*Then my mind spun a new theory. Perhaps when prostate cancer put David's sexual function out of order for a few years, he married his ex out of desperation. People did crazy things when facing a life-threatening disease. In that case, I guess it could be true he actually married her. If so, he probably left her when he re-connected with me. Yes, that seemed plausible.*

Four hours of ugly crying and implicating-but-uncertain discoveries later, I had to do something. Just something. Anything! *I should get on a plane headed north*, I thought. *Would going there help?* I paced frantically walking from family room to kitchen then back again. *Well, going to David's house couldn't make it worse*, I tried convincing myself. *Still, do you just knock on someone's door and ask if that person is still alive? If he was dead, his sons would probably just look baffled, wondering how the fact of their father's death had slipped my mind.*

*Even worse, if they said he was living then what would I say? "That's fantastic! Could you be a dear then and send him to the door?"*

*Or worse, what if an alive David came to the door, what would I say? Would I point at him and yell, "Ah ha! You ARE walking and breathing! How dare you?!"*

Exhausted, I sat down with my computer again. I tried to organize my mind, but my head was only ornamental, apparently. After unsuccessfully trying to remember how to book a flight, I pulled the cork out of a bottle of Malbec. Pouring into a water glass, I filled the glass to the brim with the wine. In one movement I tipped the burgundy liquid down my throat. Then I filled the water glass again.

That's when I stopped pacing and started talking to myself aloud, "This sucks! How the bloody hell am I supposed to figure this out when I'm completely gobsmacked by this insanity? Bloody insanity, I tell you. What I need is a plan."

With the second tumbler of wine in-hand, I started to pace again.

"What can I do? What can I do? A plan? Something. But I can't think and now I'm cocking it up even worse by getting pissed on a bottle of Malbec THAT DAVID BOUGHT!"

As I sat back down, I screeched, "Bullocks!" and then laughed louder than was natural.

A moment later, I sprang back to my feet then headed straight into my bedroom. Still fully dressed in my work clothes, I climbed into my bed. After scavenging in my nightstand, I swallowed an old sleeping pill and chased it with the rest of the wine. Lying back, I pulled my comforter over my head. My last coherent thought before I plummeted into a chemically-induced sleep was:

*There is no template for behavior when you find out your dead fiancé might be alive and living with his wife.*

# Premeditation?

## Chapter 9

The morning after the British invasion, I awakened. Then I remembered who I was and what was happening, and pain roared back to life in my head, radiating down to my gut. Fueled by a groggy grief, my first thought was: *Yes, I need to get on a plane. Then, I need to buy a gun.*

Sitting up suddenly, I shook my head as though to erase the shameful thoughts. My hasty movement startled Meatloaf, who had been asleep on the other pillow in my bed. Still in my stale, wrinkled skirt, button up blouse, and panty hose from the day before, I shuffled into the bathroom with Meatloaf trotting dutifully behind me. My head throbbed and my tongue felt fuzzy.

I stared at the bedraggled face with red, swollen eyes looking back at me from the mirror. She looked so old. And broken. And—with tangles of hair sticking out in impossible directions—she looked more than a little crazy.

*Was this the breaking point I'd been carefully avoiding for years? After barely holding it together for so long, finally had life escaped my grip?* I looked down at Meatloaf who was staring up at me curiously. Uncertain what crazy people do after they realize they are crazy, I reached for my teal toothbrush with its haphazard bristles. Squeezing from the thick middle of the toothpaste tube, I squirted it onto the scraggly toothbrush. Then the taboo train of thought picked up again. *Where would I even buy a gun? I wonder if I can find a gun store on Yelp?* That seemed likely.

I started brushing my teeth, at first sluggishly then a bit too aggressively. As the toothpaste turned into a white froth, I made a toothy grimace at my mirror self. Thinking I looked like I had rabies, I made a low growl.

"Now that's scary," I said, spraying bubbles of toothpaste on the mirror. I spit the rest of the toothpaste into the sink. Meatloaf just kept staring at me. *Was that pity in his big brown eyes?* Rinsing the toothpaste down the drain with cold water, I thought: *Then it'll take, what, like five minutes to fill out a firearms application. Oh, hmmm, but I think you have to wait like three days before they give you the gun. Will I have to wait 3 days to get the bullets, too?* I wondered.

"Humph. What difference does it make? Am I going to just throw the bloody bullets at him?" I said aloud.

Drinking tap water from my cupped hand, I spit into the sink again. *No jury would convict me under these circumstances, would they?* Although I wasn't sure what officially constituted premeditation, I've learned from crime dramas, I was likely in dangerous territory. *For now, I would just forget I thought that. Yes, that's what I would do. There were no witnesses to that thought except my dog and Meatloaf would never snitch!*

"Would you, Meatloaf? Good boy," I said, patting the downy curls on his head.

*Then there's the teeny issue of me not knowing how to shoot a gun. Really, I should probably take a class or something. Lordy, that could take months! Months!! Ugh, even in my foggy state, I was fairly certain taking a firearms class would qualify as premeditation.*

"Damn," I said, quietly.

Meatloaf looked at me quizzically.

"What am I supposed to do? What, Meatloaf? What?"

With Meatloaf staring silently back at me, I fought down a fresh wave of panic. Grasping for other viable options and finding none, I started bawling again.

After the worst of the ugly, chest-heaving sobs eased up, I called my best friend, Nolan.

"Help me figure out what to do," I pleaded.

"Are you okay, Sloane?"

"No. No, not at all. Yesterday Tom told me David is alive."

"What the hell?"

"That's not all. It's worse. He's probably married, too."

"No way. No, Sloane, that's just not possible. No. Your ex is just causing trouble. You know in your heart of hearts that simply is not true."

"That's what I thought too but online there are wedding pictures. I don't know. I can't think. I'm too confused to figure out what's real."

"That just can't be. Tom is an ass," Nolan said emphatically.

"Yes, he is but why are there wedding pictures? Help me figure this out."

"Of course, I will help. Let me do some research online then I will call you back in just a few minutes."

Click.

I felt a little dizzy. *When was the last time I ate?* I couldn't remember. I opened the refrigerator—string cheese, orange juice, leftover soup. My stomach churned in protest.

"Gross," I said, closing the refrigerator then opening the freezer.

*Maybe vegetarian corn dogs; why can't they make all vegetables taste like county fair food?* I wondered. When I spotted the green box of corn dogs, a fresh wave of nausea washed over me. Since my hands were shaking too, I really did need to eat something. After ruling out some other unappealing options, I reached for a pint of Ben & Jerry's Americone Dream ice cream. After popping the lid off and leaving it to drip on the counter, I pulled a serving spoon out of the drawer. I took a heaping bite of the caramel and chocolate-y waffle cones tucked in creamy ice cream. *Thank God, this still tastes good.* I looked at comedian Stephen Colbert's picture on the side of the ice cream container.

"God bless you, Stephen Colbert, and your wise buddies, Ben and Jerry," I said with a tap of my big spoon on the carton's side.

So, I tried to soothe my Americone nightmare by shoveling more Americone Dream into my mouth.

"Please, please, please let Nolan find out none of this is true," I begged aloud to the mostly empty room. *It just can't be true. If it's not true, then I can just keep feeling sad about the man I loved dying.* Meatloaf nuzzled my leg. Absentmindedly, I bent down and picked him up.

"Isn't that sad, Meatloaf, that the best possible outcome here is my fiancé being dead?"

Meatloaf just stared at me with his big, brown eyes then rolled over in my arms so I could scratch his belly. I indulged him for a moment before setting him back on the floor. *What if it is true?* I thought, my face reddening. *This is beyond humiliating! Even so, what could I even do about it?* I wondered.

When a portion of the container's bottom was peeking through the small bit of remaining ice cream, my phone buzzed. It was Nolan.

"Okay, I don't know exactly what's going on but whatever it is, it doesn't look good," explained Nolan.

The tone in Nolan's voice confirmed all my worst suspicions.

"I feel so humiliated. There's part of me that wants to run and hide but mostly I just want to kill him!   Seriously! He's supposed to be dead anyway. Shouldn't someone put that right? Hell, I could catch a plane later today. Yep, maybe I should just show up on his porch and say, 'There's clearly been a mistake and I'm here to fix it,' then just shoot the lying son of a bitch in the face!"

There was just silence from Nolan.

"Oh no! No! A quick death is really too good for him! Seriously, what kind of person does something like this!?

"I really have no idea," Nolan interjected. "It's horrible. It really is, if all of this is true. But let's not jump to conclusions until we have some solid facts. We will get through this, my friend.

After a moment's pause, Nolan continued, "Not to mention, with you being a professor and all, if you shot someone in the face that'd likely put a big dent in your career."

"I don't have to be a professor. I could be a yoga instructor!" I fumed.

"Sloane, you've only done yoga twice in your life so…"

"Ok, so not a yoga instructor. I could be a nail technician! Or a bounty hunter!"

"All of those sound very promising, sweetheart, and I have no doubt that all 5'2" of you would make a very intimidating bounty hunter. First, though, I think we need to find out the whole truth," soothed Nolan.

That's when Nolan made me promise three things:

  I would hire a private investigator to get some facts

  I would NOT get on a plane headed north

  I would not drown myself in a vat of Ben & Jerry's Americone Dream ice cream.

I told her I would do what I could do but I was not certain I could stick to my promise about the Ben & Jerry's.

Starting at the top of the list, I Googled private investigators in the area near David's house. Choosing the P.I. with the address geographically closest to David's address, I dialed. Although it was only 7:00 A.M. in the P.I.'s location, a deep, gravelly voice calling himself Max answered before the first ring ended. P.I. Max had a slow, measured way of speaking. He sounded as if John Wayne and James Earl Jones had produced some sort of impossible love child.

In a rapid stream I poured out the story as I knew it, "My fiancé, who lives in your town, supposedly died a couple of months ago, but I have reason believe he could be, well, not dead. If he is alive, I don't know if he's like getting ready to die soon or if he's just prancing around all working and doing stuff. Also, there's a possibility he may be married. Or maybe he was in a play about eloping but probably not. Could you find out?"

"Of course, I do these sorts of things all the time," Max explained in his steady, booming voice.

Then he proceeded to ask a long list of questions like did I need pictures? Once the laid-back interrogation was complete, I put his $500 retainer on my MasterCard.

After a pause presumably to enter the credit card information, he said, "Thank you." Then, "By the way, there is a fast way, you know, to find out if he's dead yet. See, I'm not here just to take people's money," said the man who just accepted my $500.00.

"It's something you could do yourself," he said. Then Max told me what I needed to do.

# Dead Man Working
## Chapter 10

According to P.I. Max, I needed to call the place David used to work and do an employment verification.

As Max explained, "Just use a phone with an unfamiliar number and, using a fake name, tell human resources you need to do an employment verification for David Langer. Credit card companies and mortgage lenders do them all the time. Then they will tell you if he still works there."

In following P.I. Max's instructions, first I needed a fake name. While driving, I called to consult Nolan. Without saying "Hello", Nolan said Peter and Sean were up to speed already on the current situation. Then, she held my call to conference in the guys.

"We're queer and we're here," said Peter in lieu of a greeting.

"So, Nolan said she told you about the world's biggest vag'?" I responded.

Making a derisive guttural noise, Nolan said, "Ugh, don't use female genitalia as a putdown."

In Nolan's career, she held the civilian Airforce rank equivalent to that of a Colonel. Working in that context, she'd developed the sensitivity of someone who'd spent 20 years of her life competing almost exclusively against men, Nolan said with an exasperated sigh, "It's hard enough being a woman without people dissing our junk."

Peter launched in, "Nolan is right, hon-ey! He's not a vag' but a fucking prick; and not a big one either! I'm talking one of those teeny, tiny, little cocktail wiener dicks like something you breeders hand-out on toothpicks at parties."

Hooked by the digression, I said, "Your people don't put little wieners on sticks?"

"No," answered Sean definitively. "We don't live like barbarians."

Peter continued, "And I don't care if you dip it in homemade BBQ sauce and serve it on a platter, I just don't have any use for tiny wieners…"

"Said the man whose name is a synonym for 'penis'," laughed Sean

"Well then, I'm pretty certain that makes me the Grand High Poohbah on all things phallus-related," said Peter.

Nolan interrupted. "Back to the fuck-tastrophy at hand, sirs."

Peter flapped, "Oh yes! Ya'll, we have to come up with a plan. Well, first we need some facts, then a plan." After a pause, Peter continued, "Or do you want to do the plan first? Sloane, honey, I just don't know. I'm new at this."

Sean suggested Peter give me a second to talk. Seizing the opportunity, I explained our first order of business: coming up with my alias for my new spy assignment given by P.I. Max.

Sean asked, "Well, what are we going for here? 007? Suave? Long and difficult to pronounce? Funny?"

Nolan suggested, "Ima Dike? Jane Ho? Emma Perv?"

Peter made a reprimanding, "Tsk, tsk," sound.

Sean suggested, "Anabelle? Harper?"

Peter interrupted, "She needs something simple enough that it doesn't sound made up but is also easy to forget, like Sean's mom's birthday."

I imagined Sean glaring at Peter.

"I think Sloane looks more like a 'Zoey' or a 'Brooklyn," Nolan added.

"She will be on the phone; they won't see what she looks like," Sean said.

"I say we keep it simple. My brain is fried from all this and I need to be able to remember it," I cautioned.

"Sarah? Alice? Nolan continued.

"Mary?" suggested Sean.

"You want her to be named after a biblical whore?" Peter asked.

"You know very well my mom's name is Mary."

"Um hmm," retorted Peter.

Nolan said, "It should be gender neutral in case they tell David so-and-so called.

"And not too long," I added.

"How about Mason?" Sean offered helpfully, "Mason Murray."

After a pause, I shrugged and said, "Mason Murray it is then. Pleased to meet you."

As I walked into the cool light of the big box electronics store, my palms felt clammy. *Am I walking too fast? God, why am I nervous? I am not going to steal the disposable cell phone. I just need to ask where to find one. Besides, it is important I practice my new alias. That's just good planning,* I thought.

I walked up to a gangly guy in a name tag.

"Hi, I'm..." and then I couldn't remember my spy name. It started with "M". To buy time, I smiled. Then trying not to sound panicked I blurted, "I'm Murray."

"Your name is Murray?" he asked raising an eyebrow.

"Yep, sure is. I was named after my dad's step-grandpa, on his mom's side." *Just stop talking*, I thought.

I told him what I was looking for and he said, "Oh, a burner phone."

"A what?" I asked.

"A burner phone - it's what police officers call disposable cell phones because criminals use them."

"Okay, perfect. Then I will take one burner phone to go, please."

Raising his eyebrow again, he walked to a nearby set of shelves.

The awkward guy handed me a white box with a clear top, "This one is a flip phone so it's simple to use and cheap."

Clearly, I didn't look like I was ready for the fancy burner phones yet.

Once back at home, the only thing left to do was to call David's workplace. The moment felt weighty, as though it needed some kind of ritual or blessing. When nothing suitable came to mind, I dialed David's former/possibly current company's 800 number. An electronic voice answered. *Friggin' irritating automated menus!* I thought. I waded through the menu until I pressed "4" for human resources.

As the phone rang, I repeated, "Mason Murray. Mason Murray. Mason Murry," under my breath.

Then my call rang into a voicemail box for someone named "Betty." I pushed the red minus symbol on the phone to end the call. I stood up, turned my head to crack my neck then walked to a nearby cabinet. I pulled out an oversized gas station plastic cup, the kind that lets you get 39 cent refills if you ever remember to bring it with you. I'm pretty sure I got a total of one $0.39 refill. *Crafty genius gas station soda marketing people!* I thought. After filling the cup with water from the faucet, I sat the full cup of water down next to the sink then rubbed the back of my neck, distracted. Forgetting the water, I walked back over to my burner phone.

When I dialed the company's number this time, I pressed "0" for the operator. Very precisely I said, "Hello, my name is Mason Murray. I'm calling to do an employment verification for David Langer."

The receptionist replied, "Oh yes, Betty handles employment verifications."

Before she could transfer my call to Betty's line, quickly I explained Betty was not available when I tried her line earlier.

"Is there anyone else that can do an employment verification?"

"Well, let me see if Betty is around somewhere." Then she put me on hold.

After a few minutes, a woman named Lisa picked up the line and said, "Can I help you?"

I repeated my line about the employment verification.

"What's an employment verification?" Lisa asked.

*Oh no!* I thought. Having no choice but to play it through, in a peppy voice I explained, "An employment verification is just a check to see if the person being verified is currently employed at this business." I paused and then just asked directly. "Is David Langer employed at this company at this time?"

"Oh," said Lisa, seeming to understand now. "Yes. Yes, he does work here at this time."

"I appreciate your assistance. Thank you, Ms. Lisa," I said in super spy Mason Murray's most professional tone.

After pressing the red minus sign, I sat, stunned. Slowly, I closed the phone. The next moment, I sprang to my feet, bolted down the hall to the bathroom, and was violently sick.

# Hurricanes and the Unnatural Disaster

## Chapter 11

The next day, a Wednesday, the university offices buzzed with discussion of Irma, a category 5 hurricane scheduled to hit Florida at the week's end. Living a couple hours inland, our experience would be that of about a category 3 level hurricane. Originally from the Midwestern U.S., I understood very little about the different categories of hurricanes. Consequently, I assessed the severity of anticipated storms by how worried people raised in Florida sounded when they discussed them.

Apparently, the deceptively harmless-sounding Hurricane Irma was not going to be harmless at all. In our staff meeting, one colleague suggested to the group that anyone still needing to fill their car with gas or needing to buy water and batteries leave work early today to do so. Since it was only Wednesday and the Hurricane was not expected until the weekend, I was taken aback by this.

"Why do I need to buy water? And besides flashlights, what else do I need batteries for?" I asked.

"Sometimes the power goes out and occasionally the tap water becomes undrinkable. So, you need about a week's worth of canned goods and water as well as batteries for flashlights and fans."

Since in our area, September days averaged about 93 degrees Fahrenheit, another colleague added, "When the power goes out and you can't open the windows because of the hurricane, it gets uncomfortable."

You could always spot a Floridian by the way they talked about temperature. For instance, to a native-born Floridian, 95 degrees with no breeze nor access to outside air was "uncomfortable." In winter, when temperatures dropped below 60 degrees locals added, "Stay warm!" to their goodbyes.

"How long do bad hurricanes knock out the power?" I asked.

"Depends," replied a colleague. "Last bad one I remember, it was out for over a week."

Concerned but trying to lighten the mood I said, "They really should make Northerners go through orientation or something before they let us move to Florida."

My colleague smiled sympathetically, "Oh, and refill any prescriptions you have. You don't want to be stuck for days without medicine if you need it."

Since my little curly-haired dog would be waiting out the storm with me, I asked, "Where do dogs go to the bathroom when there is a hurricane?"

Although a couple colleagues looked surprised, one simply said, "Outside."

"But what if it's too hurricane-y to go outside. My dog is little and round; he might just blow away."

"Then in a pinch, let him go in the garage," my colleague added.

*Awesome. So, my life was going to shit, my dog would be pooping in the garage, and little Meatloaf and I would be stuck in a dark, sauna-like house for a week eating baked beans and pineapple tidbits straight from the cans. Why does the Universe hate me?* I wondered.

After the meeting, I heeded my colleagues' advice and left campus to fill my car with gas and then to refill my A.D.D. medication. Although not really in a state of mind for planning, I assumed I could do both and still grab a sandwich before heading back into the office for the afternoon.

At the gas station, lines of cars stretched from each pump, through the gas station parking lot, and continued down the street for about 7 car-lengths. With still four or five days to go before the hurricane, a long line at the gas station was not a good sign. Even so, the other people in line were polite, taking turns in the cue and waving in the rearview mirror as thanks to other drivers. I interpreted this civilized behavior as an indicator that it wasn't yet time to panic. Finding solace in the fact we had not yet descended into some kind of hurricane-Armageddon madness, I relaxed my shoulders.

After 40 minutes of waiting in the car line followed by a rushed 60 seconds at the gas pump, my car's tank was full. With a drugstore on almost every corner, I anticipated a faster stop at the pharmacy. Despite their abundance, the pharmacy's frazzled employees bustled behind the counter serving an absurdly long line of customers. When it was my turn to drop off my prescription, I asked the dreary-eyed pharmacy technician how long it would be if I waited.

"About 45 minutes," he answered. "We will page you on the intercom when it's ready."

*Excellent. That gave me time to pick up hurricane supplies.*

Rather than using a small, plastic shopping basket, I pulled one of their diminutive shopping carts from the tiny cart corral. As I surveyed the bottled drinks isle, well-ordered, fully stocked soda and juice sections emphasized by contrast the large gap where water was typically shelved. Only one sad bottle of citrus-flavored Perrier sat on the shelf nearest the floor. *Bubbles or no, I needed water,* I thought as I snagged the lonely bottle of Perrier. Even more desolate, the battery section was empty except for a hand-written note taped to one of the shelves which read: *We are completely out of batteries and flashlights until next week's shipment.*

Well, I was fairly certain the one flashlight I owned had batteries in it already. In an effort to feel more prepared, I walked up and down several other aisles looking for anything that might be useful in a hurricane. In the fan section, only electric-powered fans were still in stock, which are not particularly useful without electricity. Despite the availability of electric fans, battery-powered fans of every size and color were sold out. After searching more aisles, all my cart contained alongside the Perrier was one dog rawhide chew and a box of my favorite Godiva chocolates. With nothing useful left to buy, I went back toward the pharmacy. There I waited - for medicine, for information, for a hurricane.

# Irma's Revenge

## Chapter 12

While still sitting in the pharmacy waiting area, I pulled my journal out of my purse. After opening the cover, I turned to a fresh page and wrote:

*Today is Wednesday. T minus four days until Irma comes to town.*
*Since I verified David's employment at the job he supposedly quit months ago, it is a fact David is only pretend-dead and apparently well enough to work. The ass does not even have the decency to be fully-dead or at least near-dead. No confirmation yet from P.I. Max on a marriage license for David and his alleged wife.*

Since I knew David went so far as to fake death, it seemed likely he was married as well. My logic was if a person intentionally does one unsavory thing, this meant they were equally as likely to have done a second unsavory thing as well. While my intellect felt confident in this, my emotions could not be convinced.

In the pharmacy waiting area, I coughed to distract the tears already filling my eyes. Needing a bigger diversion, I got up and asked the pharmacy tech how much longer until my prescription was ready. Looking agitated, the pharmacy tech assured me they were working as quickly as they could, but it could be a while longer.

I returned to my seat, still antsy. Needing to busy my hands, I reached into my purse and pulled my journal back out onto my lap. Suddenly, I remembered how college-aged me dealt with strong emotions. As an undergraduate, when upset, I wrote super hero spoof stories starring my close friends and I as the main characters. It was a bit asinine but come to think of it, so was my life. With that, I started writing.

Go Team 2<br>Irma's Revenge

By Sloane Noah

The universe is made up of ebbs and flows, actions and corresponding reactions. Just last week Hurricane Harvey took a dump on the Southern U.S. This week, deceptively docile-sounding Hurricane Irma is headed this way and boy is she pissed!

As Harvey wielded his own personal brand of terror in rainstorms, flooding, and gale-force winds, another less natural disaster occurred. It started when Dr. Design, a long-retired crime-fighter, received staggering news about her recently deceased fiancé. The unprecedented shock of this triggered far-reaching consequences —confusing the wise, shaking the very foundations of civilized life, and ultimately driving Dr. Design from her long-anticipated retirement of predictable boredom.

This extraordinary news reached Dr. Design via a douche-monk turned informant.

Douche-monk

/doosh məNgk/

Noun

• a crafty, shady creature prone to deception, rouses, hoodwinks, and general bad decision-making. Commonly disguised as human males, the most dangerous among these dons the "nice guy" façade. With this unassuming veneer, these diabolical villains lull prey into a false sense of security, rendering said victim emotionally defenseless before stealing their vital core, the source of all feminine joy, self-esteem, and wit.

Dr. Design was uncertain information from this source could be trusted since douche-monks were notorious for their wily and rabblerousing nature. This douche-monk, in particular, was more suspect than most because this dubious character was one of the chief suspects for being the elusive and clandestine leader of the douche-monks. Uncovering and dismantling douche-monk leadership was a job for another time, though.

Despite the paradoxical nature of accepting information from this disreputable character, Dr. Design found herself moved by this douche-monk informant's conviction. For a moment, Dr. Design paused to mentally analyze this newly acquired information.

As straightforward as it was shocking, the douche-monk's account indicated David Langer, Dr. Design's recently deceased fiancé was not deceased at all but instead alive, married, and maintaining a secretly toxic existence in the Midwestern U.S. After listening to this news regarding her possibly un-dead and matrimony-accused fiancé, she dismissed the douche-monk informant. Then, like an old neon sign, Dr. Design's long-dormant covert crime-fighting training flickered to life.

Without a moment's hesitation, she removed the dusty cover from her Smith Corona Mega Processor 5000, a vintage electronic relic from a brief era starting after the world left behind typewriters but before experiencing the technological marvels of portable computers. The Doctor admired the fine, mechanical masterpiece. The Smith Corona Mega Processor 5000 featured a typewriter's individual key strike printing combined with a viewing screen and memory slightly larger than those of a basic calculator. Together, these allowed the user to enter and save small amounts of information. Then, when the time was right (usually when unsuspecting downstairs neighbors slept), the user guided the machine into print mode. Instantly, a rapid series of type hammers stampeded information onto individually fed sheets of paper. Before being swept away with nostalgia, Dr. Design opened the Smith Corona's plastic hood. Then, with the assistance of a paperclip, a dime, and a small pink tin box of Hollywood Fashion Secrets double-sided tape, she went to work on the notorious relic.

Within minutes the Smith Corona Mega Processor 5000's

makeover was complete. From this newly revitalized yet still unassuming machine, Dr. Design rapidly searched, printed, and organized a Pendaflex Portafile's-worth of online research. With her trusty Pendaflex in one hand and her Milwaukee Drill Case in the other, Dr. Design sprang into action to serve again as the brute force and a behind-the-scenes mastermind, fighting for the side of good against the forces of evil.

After retrieving her black, Lycra unitard and leather gloves from the back of her closet, Dr. Design made a few urgent calls and texts to potential recruits and Go Team 2 was born. The first contact made was with The General. The General—actually only a Colonel but that name was still taken by the chicken guy—came aboard without hesitation. Entrenched in the military, The General was gifted at weapons and equipment acquisition as well as logistics planning.

Next, Cutter joined the ranks. With his keen medical skills and penchant for making medications and other potions, he was ready to mix, slice or dice to ward off the forces of evil. Closing the circle was Mastercraft, gifted at creating impromptu emergency structures with locally sourced, VOC-free materials. While each unique, the Go-2 members shared a passion for truth, justice, and fighting evil in all its forms. And so, Mission: Irma's Revenge began!

Before meeting at the newly established Go-2 HQ at 0800, each prepared in solitude. With logic, organization, and efficiency, The General obtained and inventoried weapons and supplies, mapped out a series of strategic locations, then, as an afterthought, borrowed a handful of change for tolls from her offspring's nearby piggybank. After The General arranged her glossy dark hair into a neat ponytail, she dashed out of the door in a state of prepared confidence, with the morning sun glinting off the silver eagle emblazoned on the torso of her black unitard.

Tall and lean, the one now called Cutter packed his jump bag, which suspiciously resembled a HIPPA-compliant bag of medicinal equipment. Only moments after taking Dr. Design's call, Cutter placed an online order using a little-known branch of Amazon, Amazon Super Prime, which meant…

*Ding-Dong,* the package was there.

With one hand sewing his oversized scalpel emblem onto his freshly delivered unitard from the Big and Tall store via Amazon, his other hand efficiently prepared tasty, nutritious, and perfectly-proportioned snacks for the mission. He added medical supplies and communication devices into his bag and still had enough time left to decide what to read on the plane.

The one called Mastercraft took a different approach. After commandeering a small yet fine specimen of a Harley motorcycle, Mastercraft updated it with an iridescent paint job then outfitted the now subtly sparkly bike with secret compartments. He even specially crafted a collapsible truck-sized storage unit that, once folded, masqueraded as tail and saddle bags. He packed these with tools, building materials, and, of course, his changes of costume. After throwing in some last-minute Duct Tape and cranberry-flavored lip balm, the Harley made a booming growl as he pulled out of the Cul-de-sac.

"Sloane Noah," called the amplified voice over the loudspeaker, "Your prescription is ready for pick-up."

Awakened from my written reverie, I dropped my journal back into my bag then headed to the pharmacy counter.

# You've Got Blackmail?
# (Not starring Tom Hanks)

## Chapter 13

With my prescription and I safely back at home and my car with its full gas tank neatly tucked into the garage, time slowed. I turned on the TV. Not seeing anything I wanted to watch, I shut it off. I pulled a book from the bookshelf. Opening to the first page, I read a single sentence, closed it then returned it to the shelf. In turn, I repeated this with three other books. Irritated by my own inability to be entertained, I fed Meatloaf. Then, for myself, I scrambled eggs. Once scrambled I shook these onto a china saucer snagged from the nearest cabinet. By then, I lost interest and left the dish of eggs to jell on the counter.

By 7:00 P.M., the act of being awake was too oppressive to continue. I changed into an oversized T-shirt and climbed under my comforter. Despite continually trying to direct my mind to anything else, defiantly my thoughts stayed tuned to the all-David channel. *If David was or is married,* I thought, *there is no way he just re-married his ex-wife because that's who he wanted.* He must have married for some issue of convenience. I held firmly to my medical insurance theory. *Yes, insurance-induced matrimony is what it had to be. I doubt they even live in the same house because David really couldn't stand her. Then, while living their separate lives, I bet he told her he wanted a divorce when he wanted to get back together with me,* I thought, conjuring the storyline further. *Maybe she had some reason she didn't want them to divorce so she threatened to tell me that she and David remarried while we were apart. Maybe she even threatened him saying if he filed for divorce, she would tell me David cheated on me this whole time with her.* I paused. *If she is technically the wife, does that mean he's cheating on me with her or on her with me? I suppose wife trumps fiancé. Or perhaps the wife wasn't the blackmailer at all. What if one of their sons blackmailed David? Even if their parents remarried in name only, perhaps the boys were still happy to have their parents linked again. Then maybe that was incentive enough to threaten to expose David's insurance-marriage in order to keep him from moving away?*

*Buzz, buzz.* My phone called for my attention from the sofa beside me. Seeing it was Tom calling, at first, I hesitated to answer then, concerned it could be about the twins, I accepted the call.

"I just want to know when you are planning on telling the kids about David." Tom demanded.

"I've been thinking about that and I'm not sure they need to know at all. Are teenagers even remotely equipped to deal with something like this? Plus, Beck is just now doing better."

"If they don't hear it from us then they might find out on their own someday," argued Tom.

"I really don't see how they would ever just stumble across that information. That seems highly unlikely."

"They need to know."

"Even if I thought it was a good idea, I'm not in a place yet where I can calmly sugar-coat explanations and comfort them about it."

"Seriously, they need to know and if you don't tell them, we are going to do it," said Tom.

My mind reeled, "They do NOT need to hear this from you."

"Then it damn well better come from you."

Not seeing a way out, I said, "Okay, okay, but I need time. I'm still waiting to get confirmation on some of the facts."

"How much time do you need, exactly?"

"A month?"

"That's ridiculous," said Tom.

"Well, I may be able to do it in two weeks, but I doubt I could have all the information any sooner than that."

"Fine. You have two weeks."

By 7 A.M. the following morning, I Facetimed my therapist's office for a before-hours emergency session. Since she charged double her normal rate for therapy outside of regular business hours, I'd avoided this option in the past. Even so, this time I'd made the appointment without even pausing to consider the additional cost. If ever I needed some professional guidance, now was that time.

Having talked me through the past decade, Dr. B. knew all the main players in my life almost as well as she knew me. With the advantage of such a long history, Dr. B.'s swift yet shrewd insights consistently cut through my emotional confusion and addressed the crux of each issue.

After I laid out all the information I had to date, I asked the question I most wanted to know, "Do you think David really loved me? None of the emotion felt fake."

"I do think his affection was genuine towards you. Since it was authentic, that's why you didn't sense any falseness."

"Why, though, would he do this?"

Unofficially diagnosing in a single word, Dr. B. said, "Cowardice." She explained cowardice loomed much larger in his life than we could have guessed previously.

"For instance, if there was emotional blackmail involved, he was too cowardly to stand up to the potential emotional blackmailers as well as being too cowardly to risk telling you the truth," explained Dr. B.

"Why? Why on Earth wouldn't he just tell me the truth?" I asked.

"Apparently, he was more afraid of you rejecting him because of the truth than he was of keeping up this long deception," said Dr. B.

"Finding out about all these lies is so much more soul-crushing than having him tell me the truth in the first place," I said. "When he 'died' I thought that was sorrow, but it turns out that underneath the pain of losing a partner there is a few hundred feet of garbage and then a layer of an even more stomach-turning grief," I explained.

*This grief is a powerful opponent because it is so relentless, steadily draining strength and resolve. Without those, pride evaporates, too, leaving only a feeble shadow self behind. Not even the sorrowful themselves can respect this whiney weakling struggling to fight on their behalf. The best a person can do is wait out the pain until eventually anger and indignation show up. Until then, one's inner self just looks on at the spectacle, horrified this puny wimp is the only fighter in their corner. The existence of that puny wimp is the main reason we pay therapists to listen to our sniveling in the first place. That is because it is too shameful to let that whiny guy talk to anyone not bound by a professional oath to keep secrets.*

With that, I let my inner weakling loose in Dr. B.'s company, "In some twisted way, I think I'm wishing for David to show up and make everything alright; although I am not sure what 'making everything right' would actually entail. Or maybe I'm just aching for an apology or some sign he has even a vague understanding of the pain he caused," I said.

*When overwhelmed by pain, reducing it just a small amount is valuable. To the tortured, even a few seconds relief is a lifetime.*

"Today, I needed to get some background information together about David for the P.I. To do that, I read through over 2 ½ years of text messages—with so many loving words - between David and me. Despite the reasons I needed to read through the messages, reliving those messages made me miss him more," I explained.

"You are mourning," Dr. B explained in a compassionate tone.

"I know this is pathetic, but I desperately want to hear his voice. I still associate David's deep voice with comfort. In a sick way, I know I'm still longing for happily ever after. Then I hate myself for thinking that," I explained.

"That is all part of mourning the man you thought he was," said Dr. B.

"No doubt. Also, in the depths of my helplessness, I keep thinking about being a kid and all the endless stories of heroes and damsels in distress. How are women supposed to be strong when we've been brainwashed into thinking we are supposed to be rescued? So now I think I may hate Disney, too.  Really though, the cruelty isn't in the rescuing but at each story's end, making marriage the 'ever after'." It is vicious to continually reinforce the idea that once committing to marriage, what follows is invariably so full of bliss there is no need to even tell that part of the story," I said. Then in a mocking tone, I continued with, "Oh come save me, strong prince so we can have our delusional happily ever after!"

"Those stories do set people up for future disappointment when they are confronted with the realities of marriage and relationships in general," said Dr. B.

"No, I take that back. I don't *think* I may hate Disney, I definitely hate those sadistic, mouse ear-ed frauds!" Then I shifted back to my original point, "Even if David came crawling back now, how does someone even begin to make a graceful re-entry into a world where everyone thinks they are dead?"

I pictured face-to-face apologies given humbly to all my relatives and friends. Even before my therapist skillfully pointed out the shortcomings of the daydream, already I knew how ridiculous it was.

"Is he a sociopath? A narcissist? A pathological liar?" I questioned further.

"That's the weird thing," said Dr. B., "From what you've told me about him over the years, I do not think he is any of those things."

"Then what is wrong with him? What would make a person do such a thing?" I pressed on with two questions at once.

"It just comes right back to some really intense cowardice. Somehow disappointing you was scarier than faking his own death," explained Dr. B.

"That isn't even close to logical," I said.

"No, it isn't. He wasn't operating on logic at all. It was pure emotion." After a brief pause Dr. B. asked, "Does David know that you know?"

"No. I should tell him, though. He should at least know that I'm no longer his fool."

Afterwards, I called P.I. Max to check in.

"Do we have any news yet?" I asked, trying not to sound anxious.

"Well, yes, I can confirm another detail. There is a record of David's marriage in Reno three years ago on January 24th and the official Nevada marriage certificate is dated February 8th."

Suddenly, my voice evaporated. My mind tuned-out the rest of Max's words explaining he would call me soon with more information.

Before bed that night, I spent four straight hours reading online Psychology Today articles about cowardice and how it manifests in relationships. After my informal education on the topic, I called Nolan to sort all of it out in the context of mine and David's relationship. That is one of the great things about best friends, you can call them knowing they will contentedly join you in over-analyzing every relationship dynamic and personality trait of your former, present, or potential partner. Not only do they do this because they know you will do the same for them in turn, but also, they are genuinely invested in your happiness and well-being. They are the rare few who are truly devoted to your best interests and who support you no matter what. These are the people who form your tribe. A strong tribe is the key to survival. Well, that was true in my experience, anyway. I thought David was part of my tribe; but at best he was just some selfish guy impersonating a tribesman.

Nolan, on the other hand, has been part of my tribe for decades. Nolan was, in part, why I took the job in Florida. I've always told Nolan everything. Things didn't feel like they really happened until I told her. When Nolan called that evening, first I told her my terrible secret,

"I still want David to come back," I said.

Silence.

"In my defense, sometimes I merge winning him back and revenge scenarios together. In those daydreams, I hold David at gunpoint or sometimes using

Wonder Woman's lasso—it varies—then I force him to explain himself. During his tearful confession, David realizes the error of his ways. With that he pleads for forgiveness and begs me to take him back. And Voila! We get happily ever after!" I said.

Another pause, then Nolan said, "Oh my, friend, I'm so sorry you are hurting, but sweetie, you have to realize he is not coming to fix things. He is not even going to show you a minute bit of respect by giving you an explanation."

In my head, emotion overrode logic and I couldn't yet follow Nolan's train of thought leading to that interpretation. I asked Nolan to explain further to help me see what she was seeing. Nolan's rationale for her view on David was this:

People who pretend to be dead are not likely to just throw up their hands, surrender, and then own up to everything. He's not going to face you now.  He's not about to witness all the hurt he's caused.

People who pretend to be dead to break up with someone have pretty much resigned themselves to the idea the relationship is over between the two of you.

Nolan's second point punched the air from my lungs. While apparently obvious to people not mired in the emotion of the situation, what suddenly struck me for the first time was:

I wasn't some almost-widow to be pitied. Fate had not cruelly pulled David and me apart via his untimely death. *Good Lord*, I thought, *David chose this. This was just an incredibly twisted break up.*

In response to Nolan's painful yet clarifying remark, I asked, "Do you remember the Sex and the City episode when Carrie's boyfriend breaks up with her on a Post-it Note?"

"Yes?" responded Nolan, uncertain where I was headed with this.

"Remember how all the characters in the episode—even the police—thought it was such a bad way to break up with someone?"

"Hmmm. That break up really loses its punch when compared to fake death and a possible secret wife," added Nolan.

"My point exactly," I said.

"Yikes. Well, I don't know what Carrie would do if she were in your situation, but we will get through this, my friend," said Nolan.

"Oh, by the way, Dr. B. said I shouldn't do anymore long-distance relationships because these do not allow a person to be integrated enough into a partner's life. In my case, that gave a shady guy like David the chance to be up to all kinds of rubbish without my knowing," I said.

"Well, no fucking shit fuck. Plus, when you don't have the insight that comes from day-to-day interaction, it takes so much longer for deception to come to light. There is just no room for secrets in a healthy relationship. The way I see it, as soon as they start keeping any kind of secret, the secrets start forming a third entity in the relationship. As the lies grow, they literally take on a life of their own," said Nolan.

"You're absolutely right," I said. "The lies and secrets become the Monkey in the Middle, you know, like the game you play as kids where you try to keep a ball away from the person in the middle. As the secrets build, the monkey in between the two of you grows as well. Eventually the monkey gets so big, the two people trying to have a relationship are pushed so far apart neither of them can see what's really going on at all on the other side of the fat-ass monkey.

"Yeah, I see what you mean. I think most people just go along, pretending the monkey isn't there and assuming things on the other side are just as they were the last time they clearly saw their partner. But things change. This is where surprises come in," added Nolan.

"And you know how I feel about surprises," I said.

"Yep, and I suspect you are not too keen on monkeys now either," said Nolan.

"Oh no, no! I'm not sure you could describe the secrets and lies between David and I as a monkey. It was more like King frickin' Kong in the middle of our relationship," I said.

"It's never good to play Monkey in the Middle with King Kong," said Nolan.

"No fucking shit fuck," I said.

After I got into my bed, I pulled out my journal and wrote:

*Today is Thursday. T minus 3 days until Irma.*

*I'm still standing but I'd much rather wrap myself in a titanium cocoon and not come out until spring, or until whatever length of time it takes to stop feeling like this is crushing me.*

*Even though David was alive, somehow, I was still experiencing the loss tied to David's death. Instead of it stopping there, underneath that was the pain from feeling like my fiancé dumped me for another woman. Then to really add heft to the thing, I was facing the idea that the whole time we were in what I thought was a committed relationship, he may have been sleeping with someone else. Granted that someone else he was likely sleeping with was his wife but somehow that didn't make it hurt less.*

I stopped writing for a moment, remembering what I could about David's wife, Melissa. *I am a few years younger than she is; I have a much better job; I'm definitely smarter. Yes, I am smart, really, really smart.* I knew I was being arrogant, but I didn't care. *I'm prettier too and, hell, I even have bigger boobs!* I thought. *She's cute, I guess, but not beautiful. Was I beautiful? People always told me I didn't look like I was a college professor. I am fit. And, in truth, I'd always secretly loved my long, red hair. Yes, I am beautiful, damn it! And certainly, more beautiful than she is!* I thought with harsh catty-ness. *Why would he choose that mediocre, ignorant bitch and disappear on someone like me?*

After a pause, I shook my head as though to dispel the train of thought then I picked up my pen again.

> *Even in normal break ups, one thing I hate is the person doing the breaking up knows what's coming. With the advantage of knowing what's ahead, the breaker is already used to the idea of no longer being part of the couple long before the subject is ever breached with the break-ee. When the breaker ends it, this is all new news to the break-ee. Suddenly the break-ee has to face the idea that the person they love does not love them back, their routine of companionship is disappearing, and perhaps the breaker already met someone new. The sheer magnitude of these realizations slams the break-ee off an emotional ledge the poor sucker didn't even know they were near. Then all the dumbfounded break-ee can do is wait through the emotional free-fall. Since the fall is a long one, the break-ee has time to plan revenge scenarios and, even worse, scheme to win back the breaker before shattering into pieces at the rocky bottom.*

> *Afterwards while the break-ee is struggling to breathe and to get out of bed in the morning, the breaker has concerns like, "Hmmm, should I have the chicken salad for lunch?" Screw David and his frickin' chicken salad.*

With that thought, I typed a text message out on my phone which read, "David, I know you are alive. I know you are married. At the very least, you owe me an explanation because I do not understand any of this. And I don't want a text message or an email, I want to talk."

After I pressed send, I copied the text into an email message then pressed send again. After that, I wrote the same words on paper and tucked the folded sheet into an envelope so I could send it to David by snail-mail. Despite the obvious redundancy, now at least he could not deny having received it. That way there would be no legitimate-seeming excuse for not giving me the explanation I deserved and needed desperately.

# Poop on Slides

## Chapter 14

Before I even got out of bed on Friday, my phone buzzed. It was Max. Skipping pleasantries, the gravelly-voiced P.I. started with, "I have more information for you."

"Oh?" I responded.

"Now, I can confirm David and his wife, Melissa, live at the same address."

With a lump rapidly filling my throat, I rasped, "Thank you."

"It will be a couple days yet until I can get pictures and video for you," said Max. "I've got a few other irons in the fire that have to be dealt with first."

"No problem, I'm sure you're busy," I choked, while vaguely wondering what kind of debauchery was big enough to trump my formally presumed dead fiancée being alive and living in the same house as his wife-apparent.

After hearing this news from Max, I needed time to be miserable alone. Since it was the Friday before the impending hurricane, public schools were cancelled for the day. That meant there was no refuge at home because my teenaged twins were there. Only coffee shops came to mind as potential hideaways. While coffee shops were lovely for reading a book, they were not the best place to sob without drawing attention to yourself. That's when it occurred to me: *they really don't make a lot of good places to just lose your shit.*

That's why, on a gray, drizzling Friday morning, I stopped at a partially wooded park with an appealingly empty playground. After tossing my keys into the console, I wandered toward the vacant swings. With small rain puddles already forming in the curved, black plastic seats, I sat on the nearest one, ignoring the water. I counted on the falling rain drops to camouflage my tear-streaked face if anyone came along. Sitting in the swing, my toes gently pushed against the ground. I swung backwards then forwards then slowly back again. Swinging forward the second time, I dragged my toes along the ground until the swing came to a loose stop. Leaning my forehead against one of the chains holding the swing, I let my mind race free.

When it comes to understanding anything, there is an intellectual understanding as well as an emotional understanding. It isn't until both types of understandings agree with one another that a person may accurately claim they 'understand' or 'it makes sense.' As it stood, I had enough information about the situation to shape my logic-based, intellectual perception. Even so, my emotional understanding lingered behind like some annoying kid brother of the bigger, faster sibling, named Intellect. Typically, the kid brother, Emotion, went around doing whatever big brother, Intellect, did. In this routine, life was reasonably simple. Sometimes, though, big brother Intellect gets way too far ahead, and kid brother Emotion gets lost. As for any kid, being lost is very scary.

Despite my ongoing wish for the world to invent some kind of emotional chiropractor whom, with one crunching shove, could align the emotional with the intellectual in my head, I was on my own again trying to force these to resemble one another. Perhaps this misalignment wouldn't bother me if my mind could rest despite it. This, however, was not the case. No matter how hard I tried to think of anything else, my brain kept working overtime to get my intellect and emotions aligned.

Before my ex gave me this unwelcome news about David, my intellectual and emotional understandings both read something like this:

*My fiancé loved me and wanted nothing more than to spend his life with me. He loved me more than he's ever loved anyone. Only death was strong enough to keep us apart.*

Since my long history with David showed distance and time alone could not keep us apart long, this consistent pattern was imprinted on my core.

After the initial news of the possibly alive, possibly married David, the emotional understanding stayed exactly where it was before, but my intellectual understanding read more like:

*I am pretty sure my fiancé loved me. At least for a while I think he wanted to spend his life with me. Even so, he may have picked his ex-wife over me which doesn't make sense because he doesn't like her very much.*

Like after any loss in which you must reconcile the emotional and intellectual storylines, this process involves pieces of memory breaking off at random intervals and floating to the mind's surface for re-examination. When each of those bits of memory were first made, these did not hold much significance. With the advantage of future perspective, these mental barf chunks are useful—painful, but useful still. Piece by piece the accurate story is recreated until eventually the emotional understanding and intellectual understandings are in synch. Once this alignment is achieved, the pain doesn't stop entirely but it at least stops feeling like it's going to crush you.

These chunks of memory sometimes come in the form of words remembered or an image of something that occurred. Hindsight is a bright light that can be used to interrogate the past. With this well-lit perspective, new realizations opened themselves to me. I saw the past, as well as the real David more clearly. Finally seeing hard truths, it was difficult not to beat myself up, especially when the occasional insight seemed glaringly obvious from my current vantage point. I wondered how I even missed such key indicators the first time. My only excuse was love served as a strong filter, carefully editing my experiences on my heart's behalf.

An idea I couldn't reconcile, though, was the finality of David choosing fake death as a solution. Having spent three years apart, it always felt the door between us was open. During those three years, we exchanged an occasional birthday greeting or hope-you-are-well text message. The contact was light but enough to keep us loosely connected, if only by a thread. Considering the delicate yarn we'd carefully maintained for those years, hacking that in two by death, albeit a fake one, was as final as an end can be.

Finally catching up with my intellect, my emotional mind gave-in and accepted this break up was final and absolute long before I was even aware it was a break up. Something about discovering this so late struck me as darkly comical. A bit of laughter rolled up along with a sob, making a wet snort. Somehow, in the twisted recesses of my mind, the idea that David made this brutal and lasting choice separating us permanently seemed just as bad as the fake-death lies.

Suddenly I wanted to be that little kid, Emotion, the one in my head going through life with the simple purpose of imitating his older and wiser sibling.

Replication is easy. Creating your own way is hard. With my head sore from leaning against the swing's chain, I leaned to the opposite chain, the side facing the playground slide.

When I was playground age, I loved the slide, despite the fact that playground slides in the 1980s were treacherously tall, long metal shafts, and ready to cook your flesh upon contact. I spent every recess going back and forth between the swings and the slide. *Well, actually, that was my routine until third grade, anyway. That was because I was a third grader when my parents happened to tell us about one of their friends who was ill.*

While an ill adult was not something that drew much attention from my younger siblings, I was an annoyingly curious child. When my parents told me what illness their friend had, I asked, "How did the doctor know that was the sickness he had?"

Trying to avoid giving an over-complicated answer my mother said, "Oh, doctors just know."

"No, really," I pressed. "How do they figure it out?"

To this day, I don't remember what the friend's illness was, but I always remembered the next part of the conversation.

Seeing I wasn't going to be satisfied until I was offered a fuller explanation, my mom said, "The doctor looked at his poop."

Thinking that staring into a toilet bowl seemed an impractical way to diagnose anything, I said, "But how do they look at the poop?"

"The doctor puts it on a slide and looks at it," said my mom.

"Well, how does he know which slide it's on?" I pressed further.

"He just does," finished my mom.

Now, in the mind of my eight-year-old self, this newly acquired bit of information shifted the world as I knew it. Apparently, using their personal discretion, doctors went around putting poop on slides in order to diagnose patients. Clearly there was no way I was going to go sliding all willy-nilly when our playground slide may or may not be one of the ones with poop on it. From that moment forward, I was off playground slides.

Years later in high school biology class, we prepared microscope slides with fibers like cotton, wool, and silk for viewing. Suddenly an old mental barf chunk broke free and I realized: the doctor looked at poop on a SLIDE, on a glass microscope slide. In my limited eight years of life experience, I'd made emotional peace with the idea playground slides were not for the squeamish. Now, with this new intellectual understanding about poop being on microscope slides instead, my emotional understanding shifted accordingly. Oddly, this insight left the high school me feeling morose. The sadness, I realized, was because my best sliding on the playground days were behind me. I knew I'd never take advantage of the freedom that came from knowing playground slides were poop-free.

# Unholy Matrimony & Hot Todd

## Chapter 15

When David and I first reconnected with occasional friendly phone conversations, that's when David lied that first lie, the lie that fed all the others:

My text question: Do you have a partner?

David's texted reply: No. No partner.

Clearly the lie was intentional because, as a rule, people remember when they have a spouse.

Knowing I was blissfully ignorant and snared in David's web for so long left me feeling ridiculous. *How can I be so capable and intelligent yet still be such a slow-witted boob in a relationship?* I wondered. *Never. Never again.* I promised myself over and over. Even as I repeated the promise, though, a small voice in my head said, "While that's a reasonable proclamation, Dr. Noah, how exactly does one avoid being a ginormous mammary gland?" *Question everything,* I thought.

"Yeah, be the paranoid chick in relationships. Guys will love that," the voice said sarcastically. *Perhaps I just need to avoid love altogether?* Yes, in the playground of life, love was now my slide that may or may not have poop on it.

Even though I now knew the real, living-and-breathing David did not in actuality resemble the image I'd painted in my head of the honest, selfless man, I was still desperately attached to my mind's phantom. Even knowing that wasn't the real David did not stop the mourning. Instead, I mourned intensely for the mind-painting, the man I thought he was.

This loss cut even more deeply than David's "death." When I first heard David "died," for weeks I slept with one of David's T-Shirts, clinging to it like a security blanket. Even though he was gone, it mattered that what we had was real. His shirt was a tangible reminder of all that existed between us, a monument to what had been.

Now I was mourning a phantom, and mourning a phantom is different. Since the apparition never truly existed, I no longer had anything solid to cling to. There was no physical evidence of the David I loved because that David, the one in my mind, was nothing more than make-believe.

Even worse than the honest David being a figment of my imagination was the thought that struck next: What if honest people did not exist at all? What if seemingly honest people were simply just better at hiding lies than others? What if real trust in relationships didn't or couldn't exist? Maybe the idea of mutual trust was just a nice story to comfort the gullible and the delicate when they sought relationships. Before David's unseemly resurrection, I believed trust in relationships existed as a safe place to rest a weary soul, a bit of white space within love. Was there no white space at all? Was the safe place I believed in all unicorns and leprechauns—nothing more than fantasy?

Since I'd always held firmly to the importance of integrity, I wondered if that made me a genetic freak, a mutation, or even worse was I deluded about my own nature? Starting to spiral in my worry and fear, I called and scheduled the next available appointment with Dr. B., which was over 24 hours away.

Considering my existential crisis and its accompanying panic expanding at an alarming rate and with professional intervention a day away, I did what any normal person who doesn't have immediate access to a therapist would do. I talked to the next available human willing to listen regardless of their expertise or lack-there-of on emotional issues. In other words, I went to work out with my personal trainer and talked to him about it.

Oh yeah, I have a personal trainer. Having grown up with practical-minded parents, I used to think personal trainers were an extravagance for celebrity sex symbols like Beyoncé or Santa Claus.

During my younger life, when I played soccer and basketball and rode my bike everywhere for fun, I agreed with them. Even into adulthood when weekend bike rides were replaced by trips to the grocery store in my SUV, I still agreed. That's because in my 20s and 30s, my daily run was an active person's reprieve from an otherwise hectic life.

Then things shifted in my 40s. First, my energy level slowed, followed then by my metabolism. For a while, I even convinced myself gravity somehow suddenly became stronger because my legs felt so heavy when I tried to run. Instead of fun or a reprieve, exercise was pure, unadulterated work. When something is all work, you usually need a motivator that comes with an immediate reward or consequence. For instance, when deciding whether to go to your day job, you know that the reward for going is keeping your house, car, etcetera, and if you quit going to your day job, then soon you will be sleeping on someone's sofa and traveling on foot. So, with those nearly immediate effects in mind, you make your choice.

Fitness is different. The big goals like extending the length of your life are rewards that come far in the future and even then, it's never clear whether it's been achieved. So instead, you look for more immediate feedback. Any woman aged 40+ who occasionally gets ogled when walking past a construction site can tell you, it is surprisingly still satisfying though does not offer the same level of motivation as keeping a roof over your head.

> Side note to women under 40: likely you find it rude and offensive to receive catcalls when walking past a construction site. Officially, we are offended for you; however, this tends to happen less with advancing age and due to lack of supply of said catcalls, demand goes up (a.k.a. you want it more). As you can see, it is not a matter of losing our feminist pride but rather simply sex-appeal economics.

What I'm saying is with all the changes in routine and the unfamiliarity with the new town that came with relocation, the manipulating bastard that is my bed got the best of me and I fell out of my long-held custom. At first, this didn't seem like too bad of a thing. That is until my clothes stubbornly stopped fitting—and I don't mean just my tailored, fitted clothes. Also, my favorite blue jeans, then my yoga pants, and eventually even my period underwear refused to fit. The breaking point was one morning after I searched desperately for work-appropriate pants that fit comfortably and I ended up going to work in a long-forgotten pair of old maternity pants.

At work, wearing my khaki prego pants with their giant stretchy panel, I realized I had to do something. What, though? Then I asked myself what—*truly*—would motivate me day after day to exercise? That's when a moment of genius struck!

The one thing that would be a sufficient motivator was getting a young, (and very hot) male fitness trainer to stand there with me and tell me what to do while I was at the gym. Since I didn't want said impossibly fit, smokin' hotty thinking I was fat or weak, I would work out as hard as I could. Then while I was chatting it up with my trainer and trying very hard to look like the workout wasn't killing me, I eventually got the world's best side effect: I got more fit.

So, that was how I got Hot Todd, my trainer, at a nearby gym. Even in a loose-fitting t-shirt, his chiseled body was obvious. The second time I worked out with him, I lost my head completely and made up some excuse to put my hands on his chest to feel his pecs. Even though I was pretty certain that made me a sexual harasser, Hot Todd—who I imagine must get felt up by clients a lot—just looked bemused.

Nonetheless, I cycled back into a healthier routine. Despite being able to give the old maternity pants away and finally fitting back into my regular clothes, I decided to keep Hot Todd. This was strictly for health reasons, of course. In addition to keeping me motivated and fit, Hot Todd also became my confidant—like some shiny, well-muscled therapist, perhaps like a young Dr. Phil on steroids.

Back to my point. So that day, I went to the gym and relayed the story of my non-dead and totally married fiancé to Hot Todd.

Once I finished giving the overview of the situation, Hot Todd said, "Well, it's not weird about David being married. But fake dying? Now, that's weird."

"How is your fiancé already being married not weird? Most of the people I know that get engaged are not generally already living with a spouse," I said.

"I'm just saying, it happens," said Hot Todd.

"Well, not to anyone I know. Plus, if I'm going to be 'the other woman,' I'd really like to know. God, I wonder how often people have accidental affairs and engagements to married people?" I asked.

"I'm guessing not a lot," said Hot Todd.

"Well, I've always been ahead of the curve," I said.

After a pause, Hot Todd said "Yikes! You are going to have trust issues now, aren't you?"

"That's just the thing; I don't want to have trust issues but the whole idea of trust and honesty is really tripping me up right now," I said.

"Well, I think under the circumstance, that's to be expected," said Hot Todd, with a nod.

"So, here's my question: are there some people in this world who are basically honest? Do they exist or am I deluded?" I asked.

Hot Todd looked thoughtful for a moment.

"Think about superheroes," said Hot Todd.

"Because they will have the answers?" I asked.

"No, I mean what are the qualities associated with superheroes?"

"Tall, muscle-y, look unexpectedly good in tights?" I suggested.

"Well, yeah sure, but aren't they usually brave and honest?" asked Hot Todd.

"Well, Wonder Woman even has the truth telling lasso, so I assume she's on board with honesty."

"And there's the whole George Washington not being able to tell a lie after chopping down the cherry tree," said Hot Todd.

"I don't think he had superpowers but maybe he looked good in tights," I said.

"Not the hero thing, I mean the honest thing. Superheroes, well-remembered presidents—these are the people celebrated for their honesty and bravery. I think that's because those qualities are rare."

"How rare are these qualities though? Are they only found in make-believe heroes and long-dead presidents or are there honest and brave, non-tights-and-cape-wearing people walking around with the rest of us mere mortals?" I asked.

"Well, I think those qualities are rare, but they exist," said Hot Todd.

"You are as wise as you are well-defined," I said with a small bow.


Back at home, "Sloane, you have to see this!" said my son.

"Please call me mom," I said.

"I'm trying out something," said Beck.

"Disrespect? I asked.

"Adulthood," he said.

"So, what is it I have to see?" I asked.

"Okay, you know how I'm a 21 Pilots guy, right?" said Beck, naming his favorite music group.

"Yes?" I said.

"Also, you know I don't like Taylor Swift and if anyone told my friends that I did, well, my friends wouldn't believe them?" he prompted.

"I guess," I said.

"Well, Taylor Swift has this new zombie video which is so cool. It's got this whole vampire and snake part too. I just want to show you," said my son.

Since I was finding it increasingly rare for my teenaged kids to initiate conversation with me unless, of course, it was to ask for money, I was pleased with the sheer novelty of being included in this peek into his teenaged world. I agreed happily to watch the music video.

"It's called 'Look What you Made Me Do'," he said as he pushed play on his phone, starting the video.

Since the video started with a busty zombie, I could understand its appeal to a 16-year-old boy. Then the shot cut to a scene of Taylor Swift dancing in fishnets. Soon Taylor was reclining in a bathtub of jewels and that's when I noted the lyrics for the first time.

*I don't like your perfect crime.*
*How you laugh when you lie;*

"I hear you, sister," I mumbled.

"Shush!" said Beck.

Then the video showed a vampire Taylor Swift, dressed in blood red, surrounded by snakes. One of the snakes served her tea. *What a surprisingly polite reptile,* I thought.

*Snakes—how appropriate,* I thought, *since they are an ancient symbol of healing, rebirth, and even immortality. Me too, Tay-Tay. I'm healing and re-creating myself, too.*

Soon after Taylor Swift cut the wing of a private jet off with a chain saw, the video ended.

"What'd you think?" asked my son.

"I was impressed with the depth of symbolism. Perhaps Taylor knows that ancient Greeks revered snakes. They believed they were mysterious creatures capable of regenerating themselves. I suppose the Greeks linked snakes to immortality because they slough off their old skin replacing it with new skin," I explained.

"Don't ruin it," complained my son in response to my inadvertent slip into teaching-mode.

After my son headed back into his room, for a few moments, I felt envious of musicians and other artists. *It must be so satisfying,* I thought, *to be able to funnel your pain and brokenness into a song or some other creative outlet.* Without pouring negative emotions out in a productive way, they just stay inside of us, fermenting. It seemed much better to be able to exorcise your own demons like that. I guess that is why so many people suggested that I journal after David "died." I suppose that is how those of us not suited for writing song lyrics expel the things that haunt us.

# Talking to Jesus
## (The One that Works at 7-11)
### Chapter 16

Hurricane coming or no, custody schedules must go on.

That's why Avery and Beck kissed me on the cheek and said, "Love you! Stay safe!" in turns before getting their backpacks out of my trunk then heading into their dad and step-mother's house.

Typically, these drop-offs left me with a lingering pang of sadness each time the kids marched into their other life—the one I wasn't really part of. Even so, today was different.

That wasn't because the twins were any more or less safe weathering the hurricane at their dad's house versus mine. It was some deep, ancient mothering instinct within me that rebelled against the idea that I wouldn't be with my kids to protect them during the storm. This defied logic, of course. That is because even if I stepped in front of Hurricane Irma in my children's defense, I think we can all agree Irma would have the upper hand. Still, I ached to keep the twins with me. I longed to be the one to comfort their fears as they arose as well as being able to see with my own eyes—from moment-to-moment—that they were alive and well. Since the divorce decree did not provide any free passes or exemptions for hurricanes, I just returned the twins' kisses and sentiments then drove away, with a cursory wave of the hand and a forced smile.

Since my life orbited around my twins, I was always a little off-kilter without them but this time my typical course was really knocked askew. As my orbit quavered, it opened some puncture in my emotional state that drained happiness as my car took me away from the twins.

Without the cheerful, diverting chatter of two teens, I felt myself slipping toward darkness. Emotional discomfort is a difficult foe when facing it without distractions. In general, though, I find this unease usually passes more quickly if I just confront it instead of trying to avoid it. So, with that in mind, I started a silent conversation with myself, letting big brother, Intellect, explain to little brother, Emotion, what was going on.

"You miss the kids. You are nervous about going through your first major hurricane. This is what nervousness and loneliness feel like," said Intellect.

Emotion, preferring what was easiest in the short-term, grasped for distractions instead of listening to Intellect and facing those uncomfortable feelings. For lack of other options, Emotion tried to listen to the radio instead of feeling what needed to be felt. It didn't help, though. The commercials grated on raw nerves.

An excessively perky female radio voice bleated, "Other plastic surgeons will tell you the Brazilian Butt-lift is a 'new' procedure but Doctor had-one-too-many-surgeries-himself has been doing it for years!"

The annoying plastic surgery lady babbled on as I turned onto the street, the one I took daily on my way to work. I still needed to pick up my laptop from my office. Then my mind returned to the same channel playing all week, a channel hosting the all-David marathon.

It occurred to me that P.I. Max's news about David being married and living with his wife meant several of my earlier theories were optimistic to the point of delusion. David and his current wife were not separated the whole time we dated. It was not an insurance marriage.  For 2 ½ years, David and I planned our future together. With every long phone conversation David ended these calls with, "Sloane, I love and miss you so much." Despite the consistency with the touching words, still he hung up the phone with me then had sex with his overtly average-looking wife. Never, in all those years, did he fall asleep counting the days until he could build a life with me because he was busy already living a life with someone else.

With the radio voices making such a racket, I reached to shut off the radio. That's when I realized I was making a wrong turn. Despite taking this route daily to work for what I calculated later was 1,680 previous times, this particular commute included a total of three wrong turns.

During my last wrong turn, I pulled into the 7-11 parking lot to make a U-turn. This 7-11 was my regular go-to place for coffee and snacks when working late into night from my office. While my twins visited their dad, often I took advantage of that time if I could. Sometimes that meant staying up straight through the night cranking out research journal articles from my office. Then, when the early morning sun peeked through the palm tree in front of my office window, this was a polite courtesy from the Universe letting me know there would be no break between yesterday and today.

In part just to give my haphazard trip a sense of purpose, I decided to go into 7-11. Before going inside, I scooped up a handful of sticky change out of my car's console. After pushing on 7-11's pull door then opening it correctly, I headed straight for the coffee station. Choosing a Styrofoam cup about the size of my head, I filled it with coffee from the tall dispenser. After topping the cup with the appropriate Frisbee-sized lid, I carried the portable vat of hot liquid to the cash register. There I was surprised to see Jesus, the 7-11 Night Manager, behind the counter.

"Professor Sloane!" he called by way of a greeting.

"Night Manager Jesus!" I responded. "Isn't it way too early for you to be working?"

"Well, I'm 'Day Manager Jesus' now! And I thought you only came out at night too!" he said with a wide smile.

"Life's weighing me down a bit, so my schedule is out of whack."

"Why out of whack?" asked Jesus, kindly.

"You know, just your run of mill life problems: hurricanes, losing confidence in humanity, etcetera."

Looking at me appraisingly, Jesus said, "Professor Sloane, if life is heavy that means it is making you strong."

"Do I need to be strong?" I asked, smiling a bit weakly.

"Life is heavy then light then heavy and back and forth on like that, you see?"

I nodded.

Jesus continued, "The stronger you are, the better you can carry the heavy parts and the easier parts of life feel even lighter then. The lighter life feels, the happier you feel," said Jesus.

"So, I need to think of carrying life's heavy parts as exercise?" I asked.

"Yes, but not as exercise for your legs and arms. This is exercise for…um, what is el alma? Like spirit?"

"Soul?" I offered.

"Yes. It is exercise for your soul. Exercise for your body gives you endurance and exercise for your soul gives you wisdom."

"What if I don't want to be wise?"

"Professor Sloane, you do not get to choose these things and there is no point in struggling against what IS."

Seeing I did not have a quick response to that, Jesus continued, "You can try to push away what IS because you don't want it, but then it gets heavier and pushes back harder."

"So, I just need to carry the heavy stuff and wait for it to make me strong and wise?"

"I'd even say to be grateful for the heavy things because these will make you the best you."

"Well, I have trouble being grateful for the heavy things, but I am grateful to know someone as wise as you," I said.

"I'm wise because of many heavy things."

I counted out $2.14 in change and pushed it across the counter to Jesus.

Then with a grin I said, "Wow, only $2.14 for sage advice and a cup of coffee —what a bargain!"

Day Manager Jesus sent me out the door with a smile and a wave. With my comically large bitter cup of coffee and life lesson, once more I headed toward the campus parking garage nearest my office.

By the time I walked into the university building where I worked, it was after regular business hours. I hoped that meant I would not bump into any of my colleagues on my way to or from my office. It wasn't that I disliked my co-workers. I even considered some of them friends or at least friend-ish. Even though I was generally open about my life, still I could not bring myself to tell any one of my colleagues about how my life was currently emulating a daytime movie on a bad acid trip. Particularly since these same people just sent flowers to me only weeks ago for David's "death," I felt I'd tapped out their pity reserves already. *Besides,* I thought, *I'm pretty certain you can only tell co-workers about events Hallmark makes greeting cards for.*

Later at home, I pushed my laptop to the far side of my desk so I could write in my journal.

> *Friday, 9:44 P.M.*
> *David promised he'd always come for me if I needed him, come hell, high-water, or zombie apocalypse. Now, here I sit, staring a*

*hurricane in the face and he's 1,000 miles away, probably having a nice dinner out with his wife.*

*Maybe Jesus the Day Manager is right. Perhaps I need to focus on this as a strengthening experience. That idea is much more appealing than feeling like a predator's prey. When I feel helpless and the pain purposeless, I start to see myself as weak and fragile.*

*To think of this fiasco with David as something to grow from instead of something draining me is empowering. Besides, I don't want to be just along for a ride in my own life. I want to be the driver not the passenger so I can live my life vitally and with tenacity. But how?*

# Sentencing Hearing
## Chapter 17

later that night, Peter and Sean met Nolan and me for coffee in order to
have what Peter was calling David's "Sentencing Hearing." Peter was not a
turn-the-other-cheek kind of guy. At the very least, he thought there
needed to be some type of consequence for David's poor choices and reckless
behavior. Peter's preference, though, was for all-out revenge.

"Um, at the risk of sounding pathetic, I've never really revenged on
anyone," I said despondently. "I usually just speak my mind then move on."

"But you didn't get to speak your mind, did you?" prompted Sean

"Well, I just sent that short message, which I guess he may not have even
read. So, no, I didn't speak my mind, not really. Plus, I suppose if there was ever
a reason to take up a vendetta, this seems like a good one."

Then Nolan said, "Besides, even if you misbehave in kindergarten there are
consequences. That's how people learn how they are supposed to treat other
people. Otherwise, the world would be chaos."

"Ok, so let's start talking consequences!" said Peter, rubbing his hands together.

At first, there were a lot of ideas knocking around. Peter was keen on some
sort of public humiliation.

He suggested he march into David's workplace during the morning staff
meeting, point an accusatory finger, and yell, "You bastard! You gave my dog
Gonorrhea!"

While we all agreed Peter's idea had merit, the consensus was the punishment should more closely fit the crime.

Then Nolan told us about a dream that she had in which she and our best gays disguised themselves to look like I do.

"So, then we were four identical Sloanes," explained Nolan.

"Wait! How did Sean pull that off? He's 6'4 and has a penis. I mean, obviously, Peter has a penis too but there's at least less of a height difference," I said.

"Don't over-think it, honey," said Peter, patting my hand. "It was just a dream."

"Anyway, we all looked exactly like you," explained Nolan. "Then the four of us went to the town where David lives. Then we just started popping up in random in places David was likely to see us, like his local grocery store, gas stations, his favorite restaurants, walking past his house, or wherever. Instead of talking to David, we would just act like we were supposed to be there and ignore him."

"How is that supposed to be a punishment?" asked Sean.

"See, we kept at it constantly and never acted like we knew him. With the persistent bombardment of Sloane sightings, David started thinking he was falling into some type of guilt-induced insanity."

"Granted, we've been known to dress in drag on special occasions, like Halloween, but that is Gay Christmas," Peter added.

"Although it may not be a gay high holiday like Halloween or Marti Gras, catty revenge is still red heels worthy. Even so, I'm with Sloane on this; I just don't see David believing a tall black guy is really a short, busty, redheaded woman," Sean added.

"Fair point that," said Nolan, "but it worked well in the dream."

And so, the sentencing hearing went on. Jokingly I suggested, "Let's rent a billboard and post a warning!"

Nolan did not take it as a joke. She thought we had a "duty to women everywhere" to warn them.

"Plus, he needs to face the facts of what he's done," said Peter

"But I wrote him…" I started.

Then Nolan rolled on, "Think about it, even if his wife found out about you at some point, I'm sure she doesn't know about you two being engaged for a couple of years. Also, he started sleeping with you right after they'd just gotten married."

Peter agreed but Sean said, "That means we would have to hurt the unsuspecting wife-apparent. I don't know how I feel about that. Are we okay with collateral damage?"

Then we spent the next 20 minutes debating whether it is better to know the truth when your partner has done something sleazy, creepy, or otherwise undesirable. Peter and Nolan were adamant that the wife should know.

I weighed in, "Well, ignorance is only going to be bliss if David never does anything like this again."

That shifted Sean's stance, "You're right. If someone goes so far as to have both a wife and a fiancé, lie and cheat on everyone, maintain relationships with two families of children, and then pretend-die, I'd say there's a pretty good chance of him being a repeat-offender."

"Even if the wife-apparent stays with him, then at least she knows what she is dealing with," I remarked.

"Well then, get to it, girl. You have a letter to write!" said Nolan.

"Wait, it can't just be an explanation though. You need to include enough evidence for her to know what you are saying is true. Really it is not so much a letter as it is a dossier of deceit," said Sean.

"Ah, the 'Dossier of Deceit,' I'm not sure the truth about a cheating husband has ever sounded so fancy!" I said.

Then we adjourned. With the intention of reconvening the Sentencing Hearing at 10 P.M., we each headed home.

10:00 P.M. Sentencing Hearing Part II

Before the hearing resumed, I emailed Nolan as well as Sean and Peter a copy of the first draft letter/dossier. Once discussion opened, the consensus was the letter was clear, stuck to the facts, and established why we thought she should know about David cheating. There were only a couple of suggestions such as adding a few more screen shots of relevant text messages.

"Then how can we make sure she gets it?" asked Sean.

"Yeah, if we snail-mail it there is a good chance it will get intercepted by David and I don't have an email address for her," I said.

"I'd love to deliver it in-person, ya'll," Peter volunteered. "I'd just pop in at David's work, cause a quick scandal with the Gonorrhea accusation, and then track down secret wife-y to pass along the Dossier of Deceit."

Sean wouldn't have it, "I'm not letting you wander into a redneck construction company…"

"Well, it's a design/build…" I began to interject.

"Potatoes," said Nolan definitively.

Nolan never bothered with the full potāto/potŏto thing. Instead she abbreviated it to one word which always sounded like she'd borrowed a vegan's swearing habit.

Peter wouldn't be deterred so easily, "I'd be fine. I'm quick and crafty—like a cat!"

Sean sighed then said, "If we knew where wife-apparent worked then we could snail-mail it there."

"I'm not going to drop that kind of bomb on someone at their place of business!" I said, appalled.

"OOO, and what if I delivered it to wife-y and David showed up! Now that'd be a hoot-and-a-half!" said Peter.

"Seriously, I doubt if any of us would keep our cool if we ran into David," said Sean.

"It's gotta be the P.I. then," said Nolan. "He'll have to deliver it."

Peter wasn't satisfied, "But I really want to know what happens when wife-apparent reads it."

"Unless one of us suddenly develops the ability to become invisible—which would be really cool, by the way—then there is not any way to do that," I said.

"Damn Hogwarts for never sending us our letters," Peter conceded by way of a complaint.

"I hope she leaves him," said Sean.

Since we all knew the wife-ish person had her own history of affairs as well as never being able to successfully support herself without a husband or parental help, I said, "She won't."

"Barf," said Nolan.

Nolan never had a stomach for anyone—especially women—who couldn't get their shit together and be self-supporting. Nolan felt it was an ethical issue. "A person cannot possibly stand up fully for themselves in a relationship and do what they believe is right, if they are unable to stand on their own. If a person depends on their partner for a salary or for any reason really, a person's decision-making is always going to hinge on that dependency."

"Also, I'm sure David will try very hard to talk her into staying because he won't want to end up with no one at the end of all this," I said. "Plus, why would he leave her if being married doesn't seem to slow down his dating life?"

"Well then," said Nolan, "I think we can just assume they will spend the rest of their miserable, little cheating lives together." Nolan paused. "Then, in the meantime, we will spend our time becoming more fabulous."

Peter looked delighted.

"Okay," I said. Then looking at Peter directly, "I'm fine becoming more fabulous but I'm still not getting Botox."

"Sweetie, we are way past getting Botox," responded Sean. "Peter's been talking about getting a Brazilian Butt Lift."

# 'Twas the Day Before the Hurricane

## Chapter 18

Following the sentencing hearing, I made the suggested edits to the letter for David's wife. Then I read the final draft aloud to Meatloaf. Since he didn't offer any useful feedback, I emailed the letter/dossier to Max, the P.I.

By 7 A.M. the next morning, Max called to confirm he'd received it and intended to deliver my letter to David's wife on Monday afternoon. When it was time for her to get home from work, Max planned to be waiting there, so could he hand it to her directly.

*Saturday 7:39 A.M.*

*In addition to still doubting the general honesty and goodness of people in the world, I woke up having the regular pangs that come at the end of relationships. The most annoying of which are the waves of desperation that make you feel like you will never love again. Having trusted David completely, there is a large part of me that believes it is impossible that I could ever find someone new that I could trust isn't a lying crap-bag.*

*Now I'm just waiting, waiting on this storm to pass. At least I'm coming to terms with the idea that there is not going to be a prince swooping in to save the day. The only thing I know for sure is that tomorrow Hurricane Irma is coming. All morning Meatloaf has been acting nervous as though he knows what's ahead. Even when I opened the back door for him to go out this morning, he hung back, a bit reluctantly. Only after I walked out into the yard first, did Meatloaf—staying close behind me—follow. With Meatloaf already timid while there is nothing more than a gentle breeze and a light drizzle, it is clear the only one rescuing me from this hurricane will be myself.*

*The local weather lady said the storm will likely be at its worst for us late Sunday night through early Monday morning. How, I ask, does one petite, brainy female, even with the help of her chubby canine sidekick, stand against a category 5 hurricane?*

Since it was already Saturday and the hurricane was expected to hit the very next night, I really needed to get prepared. The problem was I wasn't quite sure what that meant. So, even before getting out of bed, I ran a Google search on my phone about hurricane preparation. After reading webpage after webpage, in my journal, I jotted the words: *food, water, medicine, light.*

Looking down at my alarmingly puny hurricane survival list, I said, "Yeah, I'm definitely going to die."

Then, I sat the journal and my insecurities aside and tried to summon enough energy to get dressed.

Before I put on my second sock, my phone rang. It was my brother, a plant biologist at Colorado State University. Even though his expertise was, somewhat dubiously, focused exclusively on cannabis, he was always comforting or at least entertaining in a crisis.

"Hey, bro."

"I want my baby back, baby back, baby back. I want my baby back, baby back, baby back," he sang. "Chil-I's baby back ribs!" he finished in falsetto.

"And BBQ sauce to you, kind sir," I answered. "Ya know, singing food commercials instead of saying hello like a normal person is going to make people think you are high."

"I study marijuana for a living; people already think I'm high."

"Fair point," I said.

"So, are you really not going to come to Colorado to avoid the hurricane?"

"I can't. There isn't any more gas at gas stations."

"That's a buzz kill. Well, don't die. That would suck."

"Thanks, I will take that under advisement. Little bro, I'm crazy stressed-out."

"I'd happily help but you, sister, live in the wrong state for me to be helpful."

"So annoying, I know."

"Since I'm a doctor, though, my recommendation for you is to drink more."

"Oh, believe me, I'm already on that," I said.

"Ah, then my work here is done!" he pronounced. "Oooo, The Shining is on Netflix! I've got to go."

"You A.D.D.-prone nut-case!" I hollered.

"It takes one to know one, sis. Smooches to you and the kids!"

Click.

Entertained but not comforted after the phone call, I went back to getting myself together. As I put my hair into a messy ponytail, I realized I still hadn't told anyone in my family that David was alive. I had no idea how they would react. *How should anyone react to that kind of news?* He's right, though. For now, I just needed to focus on not dying. To do that, I need provisions.

Pre-Irma Grocery List

1) Bottled water (fingers crossed that maybe a shipment came in)
2) Canned goods
3) Snacks
4) Peanut Butter
5) Bread

Even though the store was packed with people and beleaguered employees, the shelves were mostly empty. The scene reminded me of those pictures they showed us in middle school of food shortages taking place at the time in Communist Russia. To be fair, though, that was not the situation in every aisle in the grocery store. While useful, long-lasting items were gone, perishable and frivolous items were easily had. This meant stocking up for the hurricane was going to require a fair degree of creative improvisation.

After I got home from the grocery, I unpacked the hurricane supplies I was able to get which included:

1) Fresh cut sunflowers
2) Chocolate rice milk
3) 4 pints of Ben & Jerry's ice cream
4) Dented box of Pop tarts
5) Eggs

Still Saturday 7:31P.M.

  While I can't get bread, bottled water, or batteries, and the gas stations are out of gas, I could get sunflowers—which I think brighten up my dining room quite nicely. When you have sunflowers instead of bread and chocolate rice milk instead of bottled water, you can't help but feel the hurricane has the upper-hand in this situation. Well, maybe if Irma turns my house and I into rubble, she will also destroy this journal. That is because even though I've only had this journal for a handful of days, my writing looks more like that of a demented elementary school student rather than a college professor. So far, I've written entries in ink, Sharpies, pencils, and once with a yellow highlighter, with writing running in odd directions, sometimes even on the same page. Sentences and sometimes paragraphs are scribbled out. Also, common, easy-to-spell words are misspelled. Since I have not bothered to write on pages consecutively, there is no chronology to the entries. In other words, perhaps complete destruction of life and property would have a small upside.

Also resembling my frenzied journal-writing are the dubious health issues I've suffered over the past few days, such as excessive clumsiness, random bouts of weeping, non-functional memory, unbeatable despair, and an overarching sense of shame. Since I'd rather go into the hurricane feeling substantially more competent than I am, I wish there was a pill the doctor could give me to treat these symptoms. Since there is not, I will just maintain my carefully balanced routine of coffee in the A.M. and wine in the P.M. Sometimes I overlap the two, so the uppers and downers can fight it out—just to keep things interesting.

# Battle Song

## Chapter 19

till, I needed water. Since I learned from the grocery store clerk that there was no bottled water to be had anywhere in town, I took advice gained via the internet and created stocks of tap water throughout the house. That way, according to a hurricane-preparation website, if part of my house was destroyed by Irma, some water may still be accessible, providing I'm lucky enough to be alive to drink it.

After gathering everything from large plastic storage bins to deli meat contains, I set to filling these and distributing them among the rooms in my house. In the master bathroom, I placed two large plastic Rubbermaid containers into the large shower. These particular containers may or may not have previously stored fat/skinny clothes and/or served as a dog bathtub. (Don't judge me, this was an emergency!)

Using the handheld shower head, I filled the first container. Then I sat the second, still empty container perpendicularly on top of the first one, making a bloated plus sign. Then I filled the top container with water as well. Much too heavy to move, I left these where I filled them, stacked at the back of my oversized shower. Once all the potential water containers were filled, I tried to find something else to keep myself busy. Looking over my recently acquired rations, I decided eggs would last longest if boiled. So, I filled a tiny pot, one that had not already been used to store water, divided the eggs into two small batches, and hard-boiled each batch of eggs in turn. Then I couldn't think of anything else productive to do, so I sat down with a package of Pop Tarts and my graph paper notebook, the one I used for recording Tarot readings.

Flipping through the pages, I scanned the column that contained each question asked at the beginning of every Tarot reading. As I ran my finger down the column, I stopped when I saw David's name in one of the questions. That question was the one I asked for the reading I did right after David visited me in Florida for the first time. It was: *Will I have a future with David?*

A couple of columns over, I recorded the card that was drawn at the time to represent the present. There I'd written *"The Moon."* Then my eyes moved to the next column which was my interpretation of that card in the context of my question. My interpretation read, *"The moon represents not seeing things as they are, deception. Perhaps this is suggesting I'm deceiving myself about my readiness for commitment. The moon is a bad omen."* I had intended on marrying David until he 'died' so the first part of my interpretation was not correct. From my vantage point now, over 2 ½ years later, the Moon seemed like a very appropriate card for that moment despite my inability to interpret it at the time. Clearly David was deceiving me about his being single and certainly it was an omen of bad things to come.

My eyes moved onto the future column where I had written *"Queen of Swords."* For the interpretation, it read, *"Broadly speaking this card often represents an intellectual woman, most commonly a writer. Perhaps it represents me and my tendency to be absorbed in the intellectual world, especially when writing about my research."*

Again, with the advantage of hindsight, I interpreted the card very differently now. Whether I knew it or not at the time, the cold, stern Queen of Swords much more likely pointed to this future, my now. Was I not very grim and dour as I sat here day after day writing furiously in my journal about David? The Queen of Swords was an excellent representation of my current state. At the time I'd done the Tarot reading, my imagination could not conceive of a day where my future with David was nothing more than my writing endless somber journal entries in an effort to understand this unforeseen mountain of deception.

The next entry in my Tarot notebook with David's name in the question was the one I asked shortly after I'd found out about David's cancer "metastasizing" which prompted me to start searching desperately for some alternative cure for him.

In that reading, the card representing the present was the Seven of Swords. In the interpretation column I wrote:

> *This card represents hidden plans and trying to get away with something secretly. Also, the card suggests the hidden plan(s) will go*

*awry, revealing the secret. Perhaps this is referring to the potential usefulness of this long-hidden herbal formula for treating cancer. Then the revelation of the secret could be referring to me finding out about the herbal treatment's existence as well as the specific ingredients in the formula despite any previous efforts to keep it unknown.*

Now, my interpretation was not only different than the earlier one, but also, I was certain in its meaning. It seemed clear the hidden plan referred to David attempting to lie about his cancer metastasizing and his consequent fake death. Then my ex-husband telling me about David being alive and married were the secrets revealed. Suddenly, I felt chilled.

In the future column, *"Nine of Cups"* was written. The written interpretation read:

*This card signifies time for harvesting what is sown. Also, this card indicates enjoying life. Perhaps the meaning indicated here is literal harvesting. In other words, this is suggesting that the medicinal herbs I planted from seed will be the cure we are looking for once they are freshly harvested. Then enjoying life may come as David, once well, and me are finally able to live out our lives happily together.*

Again, the meaning, as interpreted in the present, seemed undeniably clear. It seemed the Nine of Cups indicated David would reap all he'd sown by planting so many seeds of deceit that were now bearing terribly sour fruit. As for enjoying life, was it foolishly optimistic to hope that I would enjoy life again once this was all over?

As I pondered these things, also I thought about the Tarot readings in general. The commonality I found was that while my original interpretations were incorrect in every case, the cards that came up in the readings were spot on. I shivered. Was there even a remote possibility humans had successfully created methods to tell the future, yet still failed in gaining insight from these because our small, limited minds could not open themselves to conceive of all the future's possibilities? Maybe we were like engineers capable of designing a car but even with that skill, we did not know how to drive. *At this point,* I thought, *anything is possible.*

When I sat the Tarot notebook aside, I played the Taylor Swift "Look What You Made Me Do" video on my phone. Turning up the volume as high as it would go, I started singing along. Never wanting to miss out on anything, Meatloaf came over to me and started jumping up and down on his hind legs, with his front paws reaching up to me. That was Meatloaf's way of asking for a dance. So, I stood, took his front paws in my hands, and we moved to the music.

Each time the song ended, I'd play it again. Once Meatloaf and I finished dancing to it for the fifth time, I decided two things:

1) Life is better with a soundtrack

2) "Look What You Made Me Do" was now my battle song in life

Now, I wanted a tangible reminder of my battle song—my anthem spurring me on despite the pain. The scene in the video with Taylor dressed boldly in red and surrounded by snakes shot to mind. *Yes, snakes—the symbol of rebirth and healing—are just what I need. Plus, snakes are dangerous, which makes them powerful.*

I searched online for something snake-like. I searched until I found a silver bracelet that looked like an abstract snake. Then I placed an order for my soon-to-arrive symbol of healing and rebirth.

# Little House on the Frickin' Prairie

## Chapter 20

*Sunday 7:42 A.M.*

    *One advantage of having a hurricane barreling toward you is you don't have to put on make-up in the morning. Nothing's open. Nobody's going out. It's just me and Meatloaf sitting in my bed watching the rainstorms through the window. Apparently, rainstorms are Hurricane Irma's pre-show.*

    *Since Meatloaf doesn't like to go outside in the rain, this will add another interesting dimension to this whole natural disaster. First thing this morning, I opened the back door for him to go out. After taking two steps, he started lifting his paws like he was trying to avoid something sticky. Then, he just turned around and came back inside. I guess we are going to see how long he can hold it.*

    *Even though I skipped the make-up this morning, I did put on a sports bra as well as socks tall enough to wear with hiking boots. I keep imagining this hurricane and its aftermath will be like some sort of Walking Dead episode in which I tie a bandana around my forehead and strike out on foot, with Meatloaf by my side, to find food and supplies. After that, Meatloaf and I will hook up with a small band of freakishly attractive people, a couple of whom suspiciously resemble*

*Rick Grimes (actually actor Andrew Lincoln) and Daryl Dixon (actor Norman Reedus). Then I will have to get a crossbow or learn to use a sword or something. From what I've seen on TV, it seems the best part about a zombie apocalypse is that even though I won't have access to running water or a mirror, I will look fit and amazing as I run around with all the hottie survivors.*

*Still Sunday, 10:22 A.M.*

*I just pushed a settee from the study into the master bathroom since that room is the most interior and protected room in the house. That way, if I need to spend a while or—God help me—days in there, I have some place to sit/sleep. Now until Irma or the zombies get here, there isn't much else to do.*

*Still Sunday 11:49 A.M.*

*For lack of anything better to do, I dug through a bin of old crafting supplies stored in the garage. In it I found a large ball of cream-colored yarn and a crochet hook. Since my great grandma taught me how to crochet when I was about 8, I think I can still remember well enough to crochet a scarf or something equally simple. It will be a hobby-aissance!*

*Still Sunday 12:22 P.M.*

*The first long row of crocheting is complete. Yay for my newly revived hobby!*

*Still Sunday 1:36 P.M.*

*Instead of a one inch wide and six-foot-long portion of a smooth, flat length of scarf, I've created a long strip that twists and turns in on itself like some kind of gigantic tapeworm. Since I do not have any need for a crocheted tapeworm, I have abandoned the project and re-packed the craft supplies.*

*Note to self: After the hurricane, do yourself a favor and get a hobby in preparation for future natural disaster situations which necessitate being homebound.*

Using the logic that I should go into the hurricane as mentally healthy as possible, I had another outside-of-hours therapy session. Dr. B. knew about the text, email, and snail-mailed letter I sent, each with the same brief message telling David I knew about the fake death, the very real wife, and offering him the opportunity to explain himself. Straight away Dr. B asked if David responded to my message.

"No," I said feeling inexplicably ashamed.

"If David doesn't respond to your message and take the opportunity to explain, likely he is compartmentalizing his emotions," explained Dr. B.

"What do you mean? Like a split personality?" I asked.

"No," said Dr. B. "It's just some people can make a decision and once it's made, they put those emotions away in some mental box. Then they just don't think about what they put in the box."

"How do people do that? Does that mean David doesn't even think about me?" I asked, thinking of my own obsessive thoughts about David that played on an unstoppable loop.

"While you may still come to his mind, he probably doesn't dwell on it long," said Dr. B. "Before all this happened, I didn't think David was capable of this type of thing either. Also, I suspect splitting from those emotions was exacerbated by your relationship being long distance. Really, once he started seeing you again, if he didn't leave his wife straight away, then he was never going to leave her."

"But I, I didn't know he was with her at all," I said.

"He ignored your feelings and just didn't think about what he was doing and what it would do to you in the end. In a twisted way, he may have thought he was doing a kind thing with the fake death because he couldn't bear to face your pain. Cowards can never face the pain they cause."

I stayed quiet, prompting Dr. B. to continue, "In this case, if he compartmentalized his emotions like that, likely that means he consciously made the choice to deceive you and to stay with his wife."

"It just doesn't make any sense, especially when I think about the last week David visited," I said.

*David made that last week an incredibly fun and loving week—treating the twins and me to dinners, trips for ice cream, gifts, etcetera. Then toward the week's end, that's when he told me he only had weeks to live. David and I both cried through the night. Clinging to each other, we whispered how we wanted to spend our lives together and how much the other person meant. In trying to make a lifetime's worth of love fit into just a couple of days, we said every loving thing there was to say to each other.*

*In between endearments, we talked through our years of shared memories. Always before and especially that week, David's love and then his grief felt true. Yet, in sharp contrast to that, all along he knew he wasn't dying. At the time, my sadness cut deep, but it appeared David's did as well. Was it an act? Since I'd seen him perform in community theater before, I knew he wasn't skilled enough to portray that breadth and depth of genuine emotion.*

*While certain all along, in that last week I felt truly loved. I railed against fate and knowing David and I would not have the future we'd dreamt and planned. With extraordinary consistency during the total of seven years we were together, he was always there for me. He was my guiding star, my home. At week's end, he left to catch his plane and with him, he took the next thirty years of dreams and plans we'd made together.*

"The memories of that last amazing week haunt me most," I told Dr. B.

With Dr. B walking through the past 15 years of my life with me, Dr. B.'s theory came quickly.

"Likely his love and grief were real. He grieved knowing that was the last time he'd see you."

*Believing Dr. B.'s theory, I understood logically why the depth of the emotion felt real. David and I both grieved, but we grieved different things.*

"So, the love in my Love Story was real but the story was not?" I asked

"Yes, precisely."

Then after a pause and a sigh, I asked Dr. B. for insight about that week and all the happy extravagance when David rained gifts upon us.

"What," I asked, "was the purpose of all that if he knew he was ending his relationship with me?"

In Dr. B.'s view, the most likely explanation for the last week extravaganza was that it was him trying to assuage his guilt by leaving us with happy memories.

"I don't think he was thinking straight, or perhaps not thinking at all, about what creating those memories with you and your children would do to you," said Dr. B.

"Well, it was just plain mean. That week feels like the grand finale of the whole giant lie about not being married. You know, it's like him saying to me, 'To top off my 2 ½ year performance as the loving, committed fiancé, I will blast you with a set of memories so potent that the future I'm taking from you will haunt you until it's your turn to die," I explained.

Dr. B. stayed silent.

"Another thing I can't get my arms around is how he could get away with carrying on such a long relationship with me while living in the same house as his wife. Do you think she knew about me?" I asked.

"I think his wife must know at least a little about what was going on because of the scale and the length of time the deception went on," theorized Dr. B. "Perhaps they had an agreement about having an open marriage."

"Possibly," I said, "but I never agreed to an open relationship. I never agreed to start dating a married man. I never agreed to plan a future with a man that wasn't even available!"

"I know," comforted Dr. B. "And that's what makes all of this so unfair to you and your children. You were lured into the relationship under false pretenses. That's what makes this such an awful thing to do to someone."

"The whole thing is just so cruel," I said with finality. "How am I ever going to be at ease in a future relationship when I'll be wondering if the new guy might fake die on me too?"

"It was very cruel," said Dr. B. "During my years as a therapist, I've known many, many people who were deceived but I've never seen anything so long-standing and seamless as what David has done here to you. In future relationships, you will need to keep in mind this situation with David is the exception, not the rule."

*Previously, I never held a fixed opinion on being a therapist's exception to the rule. It was then I realized being a therapist's worst-case example out of a 20+ year career of witnessing people behaving badly was not an honor I was pleased to earn.*

*Still Sunday, 4:39 P.M.*
*Well, the sky's getting a bit dark, but nothing is happening which makes me wonder why the electricity has already gone out.*

*Yep, still Sunday, 8:22 P.M.*
*Since there's still no electricity, now it's definitely dark—camping in the woods alone, slasher movie, creepy dark—and it's getting windier. The rain, though, gave way to a fine gray mist. I just called Nolan for like the 23rd time, who was out of the state for work. I told her that, without electricity, I felt like I was stuck in an episode of Little House on the Prairie. She suggested I just lean into it and pretend I was Laura Ingalls Wilder.*

*"Yes, I am just like Laura Ingalls Wilder!" I said with over-played enthusiasm, "We'd be just the same if only Alfonzo fake-died and was secretly married to Nellie Oleson! Then it would be difficult to tell Laura and me apart."*

*"Well," said Nolan, "your prairie is just a little more screwed up than hers, that's all."*

"Not feeling better," I said. "Plus, my iPhone is down to 50%, I need to go. Without my phone, I'm going to be a very grumpy pioneer."

"Just journal," advised Nolan before we hung up.

Since I'm not in the habit of going to bed before 9 P.M. I decided to take Nolan's advice. So, here I am writing on paper by candlelight like it's the 19$^{th}$ century about my 21$^{st}$ century problem.

Sunday, 8:51 P.M.

When I thought David was moving here, I bought some over-priced, scented candles that are supposed to sound like a fire crackling when lit. I thought these would be romantic to have in our bedroom. Now I viewed these candles as jinxed for romantic purposes. Consequently, I'd demoted the pair to my emergency candle stash.

Without electricity, I lit these. They didn't sound like a crackling fire, though. They sounded more like static. The scents had names that conjured up images of flannel and firelight but were overly idealistic, like Lumberjack Oasis or Cedar Wonderland Bliss. Despite their optimistic names and aromatic assets, soon my head ached. I wondered if it due the heavy scents or maybe, I thought, this most recent romantic mishap triggered some internal alarm system with which romantic paraphernalia now activated pain receptors to help keep me away from relationships and romance.

Sunday, 10:12 P.M.

Now I am writing by flashlight. I hate to waste the batteries, but I don't want to sit in the dark with nothing but the noise in my head. Also, my iPhone is down to 47%. I doubt Laura Ingalls Wilder had these problems.

Monday, 3:25 A.M.

About an hour ago, the power came back on, lighting up my bedroom like it was mid-day. Once the brightness jolted me from sleep, the power promptly went back out again.

There is no doubt Irma's here now. Boy, she's a noisy, old bitch. Not only is she making a racket, she's antagonizing the frogs too. I can hear their mad, unsynchronized croaking over the wind.

Meatloaf can't figure out what's going on. Since the electricity coming on and going back off woke me, I got up and went into the *kitchen. Out of habit, Meatloaf followed me even in his middle of the night, groggy stupor. He didn't look happy about it though. Usually when he follows me around, he is chronically enthusiastic, as though following me around is terribly exciting. Instead of looking cheerful, he wore a look of careworn resentment. Apparently, he's committed to following me around but having to get up in the middle of the night to do so really pisses him off.*

*Since I was up anyway, I took the perishable things out of the refrigerator and freezer and packed them in coolers. Yesterday I filled a bunch of those red-lidded containers that come with deli meat with water and put them into the freezer. I used those ice bricks to pack around the food. Even after repacking what I could, there were some things that just had to be left behind because there wasn't enough room in the coolers. Among the things abandoned were the four lonely pints of ice cream. It seemed cold-hearted to just walk away from them without a thought, when I knew they wouldn't make it until morning. Clearly, people aren't the only victims in a natural disaster.*

*Monday, 4:29 A.M.*

*Until I'm ready to sleep again, I'm reclining on the settee in the master bathroom but I have the door open so I can hear what's going on. Feeling like I know what the storm is doing somehow makes me feel better, as though I can be better prepared if things really get ugly.*

*Now my house chirps, creaks, and groans, periodically. It's as though it is over-exerting itself against the powerful wind in the same way a weightlifter grunts when challenging their own strength. Beyond that, all I can hear now is the wind's screeching.*

*I thought about going to sleep again but then I was struck with a morbid thought: What if I go to sleep and never wake up again? Is a person even aware when a hurricane finally overpowers their house and, with that, takes the person's life as well? Hopefully my ex-husband's house is built like a bunker, so my twins are safely sleeping and blissfully unaware of the madness swirling around them.*

*Monday, 9:35 A.M*

*I am kind of down today; I don't know if it's because Meatloaf and I slept just a few hours during the night with us both balled up on the settee in the bathroom or if it's still the fake-dead fiancé thing. Either way, we haven't yet gotten up to check for potential damage or leaks caused by the hurricane. With Irma at the tail-end of her tantrum, I doubt the winds are still dangerous but still it seems like a good enough reason for staying horizontal.*

*I feel gross—in lots of ways - though. Hot water or no, I need to shower soon.*

*Monday 11:19 A.M.*

*David still hasn't responded to my message. I thought if he had any courage or decency at all, I would have heard something by now. Instead there is nothing but a screaming silence. Since I was with David for so many years, I never dreamt he'd just ghost-out on me.*

*Ghosting is the act of one's romantic partner suddenly cutting off all contact without explanation, essentially vanishing like a ghost. Though ghosting is not uncommon, it usually happens without the added drama a person faking their own death. Nonetheless, with any ghosting, there is no explanation or final showdown with the relationship's sudden end which also means there is no closure—only unanswered questions. And I desperately need some answers.*

*In my experience, the most humiliating and painful ghosting usually follows a shared vacation or similarly intense, intimate time together. During those final days of the relationship, the one who is soon to disappear seems to make an extra effort—wining, dining, giving gifts, speaking sweet sentiments. On the receiving end, all the extra effort and expense seems to say, "You are worthy. You are special. You matter to me." In blissful ignorance, the soon-to-be-abandoned one interprets these gestures as acts of love. Oh, but those are not acts of love at all! Instead these experiences and tokens are simply a guilty conscience trying to pre-pay their penitence for their upcoming disappearing act.*

*Blinded by your own euphoria, it seems inconceivable that your loving partner is, with an impossible suddenness, gone. Poof! Just like that. Initially devastated and confused, your emotions quickly devolve into an overwhelming sense of humiliation. Since you believed every falsely kind word and act, now you feel like the world's biggest sucker.*

*From what I can tell, the whole point of ghosting is simply for the ghost-er to avoid having to give the uncomfortable conversation it would take to actually end the relationship. Since the "ghost" vanishes instead of giving an explanation, the partner that remains is haunted, drowning in their own raw, unresolved emotions.*

*And I do feel haunted. Instead of being left with gaping wounds, I deserved closure. Ghosting doesn't provide that though. You wonder. You guess. But you never know. And I'm aching to understand why David made the choices he did. Without that, I feel like I'm stuck in some relationship limbo until I can make some kind of sense of this. How can you even consider a new relationship, when your mind is still focused on un-puzzling the former one? Without the painful peace that would have come from an explanation, I'm frozen in hellish uncertainty.*

*Monday 4:55 P.M.*

*Since Irma made for a terribly messy party guest, I started the needed post-hurricane clean up. First, I emptied the fridge because anything still left in it was ruined. After throwing the food carcasses into our big, brown, outdoor trash can, I used window cleaner to scrub the inside of the fridge, even removing individual shelves and wiping every surface clean before putting the shelves back. Now the inside of the refrigerator is so perfectly gleam-y that I almost hate to buy more food and mess it up again. Maybe in the future, I can have one flawless, clean fridge to admire and another one for storing food.*

*Planning to pick up branches from my yard, I walked around my house outside. In particular, I wanted to check the small orange tree in my front yard. I wasn't too concerned about the mammoth Live Oak tree in my backyard since I figured he was big enough to take care of himself. The orange tree, however, was just a puny, spindly thing, barely taller than I was. Before the storm, it had about a dozen oranges weighing down its dainty branches. Even without wind, it seemed unlikely the tree's branches would be able to support the fruit until it was full-grown.*

*What I found in my yard, though, was surprising. In my backyard, the Live Oak was still standing, mostly. At one of its main arteries two large branches, both tremendously thick and far longer than my car, dangled from the tree, clearly torn by the wind. Also, innumerable smaller branches from the Live Oak littered the yard. So, wearing my work gloves, I hauled every branch small enough for me to drag to the curb. The two biggest branches would have to stay in their current precarious positions until I could get someone who owned a chainsaw to come over and remove them completely. Now the old Live Oak had two pale, ragged scars marking where the branches were linked before the storm. On such a stately tree, it wore the mutilations almost proudly. If Irma could do that to a titanic Live Oak, I wondered if there would be anything left of the little citrus tree on the other side of our house.*

*In the front yard, the little orange tree still stood with all its fruit attached save one orange, now sitting on the ground. How the oranges managed to hold onto those scrawny branches during such a powerful hurricane is anyone's guess. Even so, I found it strangely heartening. The fruit is the best part, after all.*

*Throughout the day, I kept thinking about the small tree. I reasoned that if the little citrus tree with branches no thicker than my fingers could hold onto its most valuable assets during the worse hurricane in decades, maybe—just maybe - I could too. The Live Oak was broken and may never be the same but trees, like people, are all different. The Live Oak was vast and high. In a hurricane those things worked against it. The wind had more surface area to grip, push, and pull. In contrast, the orange tree was small and limber. It bent while the Live Oak broke. Then one of my favorite quotes from Shakespeare came to mind, "Though she may be but little; she is fierce." At that moment I resolved to be like the puny orange tree. Hell, I thought, surely, I can at least be as tough as citrus.*

# Lords of the Ring

## Chapter 21

Once Max called saying David's wife, Melissa, had the letter, Peter took to stalking her Facebook page. As the afternoon wore on, both Peter and Sean were convinced wife-apparent would provide some clue as to her reaction to the Dossier of Deceit via a Facebook update. Approximately every couple of hours, he sent group texts to us like:

*FB stakeout in progress. No movement from wife-apparent.*
*and*
*FB stakeout still unfruitful. Are we sure wife-apparent can read?*
*and*
*FB stakeout is making me hungry for sushi. Anyone else in?*

A couple of hours later, I got another group text message from Peter saying:
*OMG! The eagle has landed!*

Then Peter forwarded a screenshot of Melissa's recently changed Facebook profile picture which now showed a picture of a ring with an arrow-pierced, cracked heart on it. *Me too,* I thought. I ached for David's wife, for myself, for my involvement in this situation that broke so many hearts.

Also, in seeing the pierced heart ring, for the first time I wondered what became of the engagement ring I gave to David when I asked him to marry me.

When he left my house for the last time, he said he'd wear it until "the end." It was a beautiful ring and I hated to think of it pawned or hidden in a drawer.

Even later still, there was another text from Peter saying

*Either the eagle is some sort of genius or is high because this is the new 11:00 Facebook profile picture.*

Then Peter forwarded us a picture showing some sort of gourmet sandwich and what looked like sweet potato chips.

The sandwich didn't interest me. Yet the earlier post weighed on me. Picking up my journal once more I wrote.

Go Team 2

Lords of the Ring


By Sloane Noah

On the screen of what appeared to be a non-descript black Fitbit on Dr. Design's wrist, an alert ticked across the secret Go Team 2 messaging system. Since Mastercraft cleverly altered these Go Team 2 Fitbits to serve this function, all across town all four Go Team 2 members received the same message.

"…*This is a Go Team 2 Alert…Suspected douche-monk is keeping over-priced symbol of love as a sardonic souvenir. Mission Lords of the Ring will commence at 2200 hours. This message will automatically delete in 3…2…1…*"

Then the screen went pale before returning to normal. Even before the Fitbit screen blinked white, Dr. Design was poised like a cougar, ready to leap into action.

At 2200 hours, the Go Team 2 members met at the newly constructed, zero-energy headquarters. Quickly calling the meeting to order, The General reported new information on the whereabouts of the ring which she collected under the guise of official military business during her most recent reconnaissance mission in the Midwest. As a result of this new intel, the General explained The Team would head north independently then meet up as a group in the Wal-Mart parking lot, nearest the alleged douche-monk, David's, house.

"Oh, good Lord," said Cutter, rolling his eyes in response to the idea of taking his Louis Vuitton shoes anywhere near a Wal-Mart parking lot.

Cutter and Dr. Design arrived simultaneously in the Wal-Mart parking lot where The General was waiting next to Mastercraft, who was making some adjustments to some sort of truck. Calling the informal meeting to order, the

General said today Mastercraft would brief us on the logistics of mission: Lords of the Ring.

Mastercraft stood, wiping his hands on a shop towel. "Ya'll, our mission here today, if you choose to accept it, first is to infiltrate this box store to obtain necessary perishable supplies. I will stand guard protecting our equipment here," Mastercraft gestured at the boxy, white truck, "while you three don these disguises during said supply acquisitions." In turn, Mastercraft handed each of us a small stack of clothing and accessories.

The General eyed her disguise dubiously. Then a whispered disagreement between The General and Mastercraft followed. Afterwards, Mastercraft took Dr. Design's disguise and traded it for the one originally given to The General.

After changing behind the truck, The General emerged wearing overly tight, camouflaged sweat pants, topped with a black t-shirt that read "Even Duct Tape Won't Fix Stupid." The disguise was set off with a pack of cigarettes rolled up in The General's sleeve and a large temporary tattoo that started on The General's shoulder and ran the length of her arm that read, "I ♥ Waffle House."

Once Dr. Design was in her disguise, it was clear why The General had made a fuss. In Daisy Duke-style cut-off denim shorts, and a baby blue button up shirt tied at her waist, Dr. Design came cautiously from behind the truck. In the strappy high heels that completed her ensemble, Dr. Design attempted a sultry swagger but looked more like a baby deer walking for the first time as she came to join the group.

"Next time, Mastercraft does not get to pick the disguises," grumbled Dr. Design as she tugged at the bottom of her short shorts as though this might make them longer.

Lastly, Cutter popped out from behind a nearby shrub. Cutter's long, dark legs stuck out of skin tight, black spandex biking shorts and his belly button showed as the pit-stained V-neck T-shirt he wore was too short for his tall frame. Mastercraft stepped in front of Cutter and in a blur of busy arms, Mastercraft added the final touches to Cutter's disguise. These included a mound of bushy fake chest hair which appeared to be trying to escape from the "V" of Cutter's V-neck as well as a bright teal fanny pack fastened around his waist.

Despite being less than thrilled with their disguises, the Go Team 2 members found they blended in seamlessly while inside Wal-Mart procuring supplies. After spending ten minutes gathering items from the refrigerated foods and adjacent sections, the three Go Team 2 members waited in line at the single open and staffed check-out station among the 30 check-out stations available. During the long minutes of waiting in line, the other 29 check out stations -

either closed or the actively ignored self-check outs—stood guard like frozen robotic sentinels.

When the three Go Team 2 members walked into the parking lot, they each pushed a blue cart brimming with white plastic bags packed with supplies.

Stopping where the non-descript truck formally was, Dr. Design stood there barefoot, high heels slung over the push-bar of her cart, then asked the obvious question, "Where's Mastercraft?"

As though on cue, Mastercraft—or a man resembling the guy previously known as Mastercraft - stepped out of the door of what now appeared to be a Brat and Beer Concessions Truck. The now full-bearded man wore work boots, Dickie's blue jeans, a flannel shirt, and a Cheese Head hat. The other three Go Team 2 members gaped at him.

Before you could say, "Milwaukee's Best" three of the Go Team 2 members, now wearing their notorious black unitards, bumped along in the rear of the Brat truck. Mastercraft still in his flannel shirt and Cheese Head disguise was behind the wheel. Over the truck's interior intercom, Mastercraft rapidly spoke describing the upcoming steps of the mission interspersed with details about local attractions.

"From the construction company's parking lot, Cutter, The General, and Dr. Design enter the workplace of the suspected douche-monk via the northern-most entry…As you see on your left, ya'll, it is the Fairbank family farm which grew the state's largest pumpkin, taking home the blue ribbon at last year's state fair…When you hear the brat truck chime, the building will be breached under cover of the brat truck diversion…Oh and on your right, notice the statue of the revered Jersey Farmer from Quebec who first introduced cheese curds to the American Midwest in 1962…"

Once the brat truck pulled up in front of the company's main entrance, Mastercraft used a complex series of rapid hand signals, indicating for the team to ready themselves. Simultaneously the truck's amplified tin-y melody rang out, the three Go Team 2 members flooded from the back of the truck, and employees, attracted by the tune indicating brats and beer were available in the in the vicinity, poured out of the building. Like zombies coming out to feed, the employees moved slowly en masse toward the sound and coagulated in front of the truck's side service window.

Little did the unsuspecting employees know, Mastercraft was topping a long line of beer-filled mugs with a potion Cutter concocted from ingredients Dr. Design acquired via her Colorado-based, plant biologist brother whom the team knew only as Dr. Doobie. Then Mastercraft's voice rang out over the loud speaker hidden in the giant brat mounted to the van's top.

"Brats! Get your brats! Buy 10 and get a Pony Keg of Milwaukee's Best free! Fresh, hot brats here!"

"Cold beer on tap! Keep Calm and Root for The Packers mugs only $1.00!"

"Giant wieners on warm buns and cold beer here!"

In no time, the small crowd was gulping down mugs of spiked Milwaukee's Best and munching on fat brats. Just as the last customer was served, Mastercraft could see Cutter's concoction taking effect.

Meanwhile inside, Dr. Design started to turn on the office's overhead lights, but The General motioned quickly, and Dr. Design stopped mid-movement. Then The General passed pairs of night vision goggles to the team. Apparently when the person in charge of equipment acquisitions has access to night vision goggles, this renders the need for electric light unnecessary.

The three Go Team 2 members moved among the cubicles in complete silence. Uncertain which office belonged to the suspected douche-monk target, the trio moved stealthily from office-to-office.

Cutter paused signaling a question to the other two which, roughly translated, meant, "Which office owns the douche-monk?"

Dr. Design signaled back indicating they should look for artifacts of ownership. With that, the team continued forward, patiently scouring family photos hung on cubicle walls with push pins and scrutinizing personalized coffee mugs. Then luck found them when they came across a desk with two books sitting on it. The first was titled "Polygamy for Dummies" and the other was "The Big Book of Terminal Illness Symptoms for Actors."

Immediately the team members began riffling through drawers and cabinets. Just when they were starting to think that perhaps the reputed douche-monk wasn't storing the ring in his office, providence provided again. Underneath an upside-down coffee mug reading "You're awesome! Keep that shit up!" they found a wooden box and inside the wooden box was the ring!

Without even a moment to celebrate their discovery, they saw the purported douche-monk target moving towards them in the dark. All three found hiding places and stowed their night vision goggles. Then, just as the douche-monk flipped on the desk lamp in his cubicle, Cutter and The General constrained the target, holding him by the arms.

In the light, Go Team 2 could see the target's pupils were abnormally enlarged. Already docile due to the brat truck's Milwaukee's Best which was, as the team knew, spiked with a university-lab-developed, high concentration of non-medicinal marijuana extract. This extract made consumers as chilled out and trusting as Rocky Mountain teens at a three-day music concert. When an oafish grin slowly spread across the supposed douche-monk's face, Dr. Design knew it was time to begin the interrogation. Knowing they had only moments before their mission would be compromised by other employees returning to their offices, Dr. Design asked the single most pressing question.

"Are you or are you not a douche-monk?"

With glazed eyes and a looney grin now frozen on his face, the target responded leisurely, "I'm not just a douche-monk, you sillies. I am The Douche-Monk Supreme!"

Then, as he cackled with senseless laughter, the Go Team 2 members faded away as imperceptibly as they arrived.

# Bizarro Pen Pals

## Chapter 22

With public schools and the University still closed on Wednesday, I tried to keep myself busy at home. That's when I checked my home email. There, I was shocked to see a message from Melissa, David's wife. Since I sent my email address to her in the letter delivered by the P.I., I knew she could contact me, but I doubted that she would.

Wednesday, 7:11 AM
Sloane,

I got the letter you sent to me. Since it was such a shock, it took me a couple days to read it all the way through. It was just too much to take in all at once. And no, I didn't have any idea there was anything going on between you and David.

I guess David isn't the person either of us thought he was. Of course, I'm crushed by all this. All I can think is that I wish I hadn't gotten back together with him. If I knew he was the same manipulative liar, I would not have. It's obvious he hasn't changed.

Although this may sound weird, I do appreciate you telling me everything you did. Even though it is as horrifying as it is, I needed to know that this second try at our marriage was a sham. Also, I'm sorry for the pain David's caused you and your children.

Melissa


Wednesday 8:26 AM

Melissa,

Thank you for your message. I really debated whether I should tell you because I knew how hard it would be to hear. Even so, I worried if I left you in the dark, David might repeat the pattern later with someone else. With that being a risk, I didn't feel it was fair to let you go forward in the relationship blindly. In the end, I just thought having facts would help you make informed decisions.

Since I did not even believe David was capable of this kind of deception, this has been an agonizing time for me as well. My heart goes out to you as you start dealing with this. Not only does it make me ill to think about how he toyed with my kids' emotions as well as my own, but also it is even worse when I think about how he disregarded your wedding vows and, with those, your feelings. Then, on top of all that, he willingly set a terrible example for your sons. How awful to brazenly betray their mother as the standard for how to treat their future partners. I believe it is clear that none of our feelings really matter to him and that he will always put himself first.

Since David knew I would never tolerate being the other woman, I assume that's why he pretended death rather than just tell me the truth. The whole fake-death thing boggles my mind. While having a wife and fiancée at the same time is bad enough, what type of person fabricates their own death to avoid telling the truth? And the fact he had to maintain so many lies for so long to make that plausible shows what a skilled liar he truly is. Since you got my letter, I can't even imagine the kinds of lies and excuses he's told you. No doubt he's still trying to avoid being held accountable.

He always made a big deal about how your first marriage ended, emphasizing how he was the victim in that. From your message, I got the impression there may have been more to it. Did he cheat on you when you were married the first time? Either way, I foolishly misinterpreted his indignation about the end of your first marriage as a genuine dedication to commitment and monogamy.

Also, as I am dealing with all this betrayal, I still don't know what the actual story and timeline are associated with David's health. Did his cancer reoccur 1 ½ years ago? And since that time, has he been part of a prostate cancer study at The University? It doesn't seem wise to trust anything he told me.

Also, I'm sure as you process everything, you will have questions as well. For me having answers seems to help, so please know you are welcome to ask me questions that come up for you. I really do hope you are able to find some peace, however that may be.

Sincerely,

Sloane

Wednesday 10:40 P.M.

Dear Sloane,

I don't even know where to start. I suppose I will answer your questions first then move onto mine.

During our first marriage, he and I tried an open marriage for a few months. It seemed like a way to keep our family together and for David to have sex as frequently as he wanted because that was always his complaint. In that time, David slept with at least four women that I know of. Also, I developed a relationship with a male friend I had at work. At first, David was okay with it. Over time, though, he felt very threatened by our relationship and insisted I choose between them. As you know, I chose my boyfriend.

Also, there's something you need to know about your relationship with David the first time, before you moved. The night before his prostate surgery, David spent the night at my house so I could drive him to the hospital early the next morning. I don't know why he didn't have you take him. Regardless, that night he tried to talk me into sleeping with him—literally he begged. Knowing he was going to your house to recover after the surgery, I refused.

David's cancer did not recur as he told you. In reality, the cancer was never completely gone after his surgery, but it didn't change for a long time. We got remarried a couple years ago. Now I wonder if re-married me because my health insurance would cover his implant surgery while his would not.

About 1 ½ years ago, they found a spot-on David's arm which we worried meant the cancer had gone into his bones. In the end, that was not the case. This year he joined a study at the University involving hormone suppression therapy; but he is still doing well and certainly is not dead.

I'm still reeling from all this. This evening, I confronted David about your engagement, but he won't tell me anything. Some things I'm wondering are: How long was your engagement? And how far did you guys get with wedding planning? He says you never showed him a wedding dress, but he mentioned it in one of the text message screenshots you sent—so obviously that's a lie. Also, he said he didn't have much of a relationship with your kids. Is that a lie, too? When was he supposedly moving to Florida?

I know this is hurtful for you as well but I'm hoping to get some of the answers he is refusing to share with me.

Thanks,

Melissa

Thursday 6:59 A.M.

Dear Melissa,

David's version of how your first marriage ended was quite different. In his version, there was no mention of an agreement about an open marriage. He simply said that he found out you were cheating on him and when he told you that you needed to choose between the two of them, you chose not to stay with David. Obviously, the implications are very different in his telling.

Although I don't remember why I didn't drive David to his prostate surgery, he never told me you were taking him nor that he stayed with you the night before. If memory serves, I believe he told me his dad took him to the hospital. Supposedly at that point, he and I were in a committed, monogamous relationship but apparently that didn't stop him from trying to sleep with you, even when I was just a couple of miles away.

Before I moved to Florida, David wanted me to marry him then, but I wasn't ready. Also, I told him I didn't think it would be good for him to move so far from your sons. So, we ended things until 2 ½ years ago.

Shortly after he visited the first time in 2015, we started talking about him moving to Florida. One weekend visit in early 2016, David, myself, and my children got dressed up and went to a winery for a picnic. It was there I asked him to marry me and gave him a ring. He put the ring on, seeming very happy. He asked if I wanted him to buy me an engagement ring, too. I told him just getting me a wedding ring was fine. In total, we were engaged for about 1 ½ years before he "died."

Initially, our plan was for him to move here in the summer before this one. He even told me he talked to you, as his ex-wife, about how to split time with your youngest son. Also, he said he talked to your son about moving here, but Chris wanted to stay in his current high school. Still, that meant your youngest would be in Florida over school breaks. So, in the house I bought and David helped remodel, we had a 4th bedroom we always referred to as your Chris' room.

As that summer approached, David pushed the move date out further to the summer that just passed. He said he wanted your son to be old enough to drive and be more independent before he left.

At first, David and I talked about a 'real' wedding with guests, flowers, etc. Later we decided we'd elope. The assumption was we would marry as soon as he moved here. I believed this May's visit was the last one before he moved here permanently. Since I was feeling spontaneous when he first got to my house in May, I asked him if he wanted to get married that week. He was noncommittal. Obviously, I had no idea David had backed himself into a corner and was at the point he clearly needed to end things with one of us.

Apparently, he decided the fake death was the easiest out so he told me later that week that he only had a handful of weeks to live. One of the sickest parts of that whole charade is that because he was "dying," we spent the end of that week very intimately, even crying together and professing our love.

Regarding the relationship with my children, while he didn't see them every time he visited, he already had established relationships with them from when I lived up north during graduate school. While living in Florida, my kids sometimes requested David to visit on certain weekends so they could spend more time with him. Also, David arranged those visits knowing the kids requested them. I have pictures of the four of us at various events including a magical tea party and other examples of "family time." Even if David doesn't consider that a lot of time, it doesn't change the fact my kids, particularly my son, are very attached to him.

With that, I've been struggling with how I am supposed to talk to my kids about David being both married and alive. At this point, I've asked two therapists for advice. Their recommendation is for me to talk to the kids as though this was a divorce. They suggested I say things like, "none of this is your fault" and "if you want to have a relationship with David now or in the future, that is okay with me and you are not betraying me by doing that." In other words, David can play-down his relationship with my kids as much as he wants but even so, my kids, myself, and numerous therapists agree he was quite connected with them.

Since you are married to him and he's the father of your children, I do not envy the hard choices you have ahead. As David knows, I left my children's father for a much smaller offense than what David has done. Because of that, I've wondered if he believed you'd be more forgiving than I if all this came to light. Regardless, as you figure out what is best going forward, I wish you strength and wisdom.

Sincerely,
Sloane

Thursday 9:01 A.M.

Dear Sloane,

Since I've known David most of my life, this situation is making me question everything. By the way, it was a good idea to have someone deliver the letter to me directly. I'm sure David would have made certain I never got it if you had sent it by mail instead.

And thank you for answering all of my questions. You are right; having answers does help in some strange way. I have one more question I'd like to ask you though. If this awful situation was the other way around and you were David's wife, what would you do?

Sincerely,

Melissa

After reading Melissa's email, I read it a second time. Did she really want my advice about her marriage? How, I wondered, could I help her when I was already struggling so hard to help myself? Suddenly I felt heavy—weighed down—and nauseous.

Though uncertain about what may be an appropriate penitence when you inadvertently cavort with someone else's husband for years, still I felt I should help her in whatever way I could. Besides, we were both betrayed in similar ways. The more I thought about it, the more likenesses I saw between us—both mothers, both love the same man, both trying to fumble through an overwhelming amount of betrayal and pain. How could I possibly find words, any words, that may be appropriate or helpful?

When I called Nolan, I knew what she would say before I even read the email to her and asked her for her opinion about what I should do. Still, I needed to hear it from her. That day she gave me the same advice we'd passed back and forth to one another for years when faced with a difficult situation.

She said, "Hit pause."

By that, Nolan meant I needed to take some time to sit with the dilemma without trying to resolve it.

We started giving one another that advice after the day I was sitting in an acupuncturist's waiting room and I picked up a book called the *Tao Te Ching* from the side table. Having already read the *Tao of Pooh* during college, the *Tao Te Ching* was somewhat familiar since it was the type of Taoist philosophy discussed in the *Tao of Pooh*. In case you haven't picked up the *Tao Te Ching* book in your acupuncturist's waiting room, it is a small book with passages about the length of a poem on each page.

From that text, one verse I read that day stayed with me. As I recalled, it said something along the lines of: when a problem or issue is unclear, can you sit still until the best solution occurs to you? Until reading that paragraph, I'd never spent much time waiting for solutions to come to me. Even so, I couldn't argue with the logic because, besides waiting, what other reasonable option is there when you do not know how to respond to a situation? Already Nolan and I knew acting impulsively had not served us well in the past. So, by the process of elimination, this seemed like the next strategy to try. From the day I read that passage while waiting to be stuck with tiny needles by Dr. Amy, we embraced this strategy.

When I finished talking to Nolan, I was compelled to figure out what this particular pause would look like. Since Taoists wouldn't want me overthinking that either, I decided just to go take a shower. Sure, I didn't have electricity nor hot water, but a shower was what I most needed at that moment.

On such a gloomy day, there was only a hint of a cool, dim light in the bathroom. Carefully, I shuffled around the settee I had not moved yet then sat a candle on each of the vanity's edges. Without electricity, I planned to shower by emergency candle candlelight.

With each candle lit and the mirror serving as a backdrop, in truth they gave a peaceful light for showering. This meant the tranquil setting was oddly incongruent with my agitated mood. *A shower would help though.* With that thought, I undressed.

In the low, flickering light, I reached to turn on the shower. That's when I noticed the large Rubbermaid containers still filled with water and stacked toward the back of the shower. Since these containers were the size you might choose for storing holiday decorations, they were very heavy when filled with water. Still stacked on top of one another in the shape of a giant plus sign, I decided I'd just tip the top tub since I couldn't pick it up.

Side note on shower design: During the house remodel, I was very particular when I designed this shower. Not only did the shower not have a door, to eliminate tripping hazards, I designed its floor to gently slope toward the drain rather than adding a curb at the shower's edge that required stepping over in order to get in and out. With that, the regular bathroom floor tile transitioned smoothly and at the same level as the shower floor's edge. To me, it looked and felt almost spa-like.

Carefully tipping the topmost water-filled Rubbermaid container, the liquid slowly breached the edge. Then with a jolt, the weight of the water jerked the plastic container out of my hands. With the abrupt shift, the container fell to the shower floor, expelling all the water in a rush—all 20 gallons of it. With the seamless, contemporary shower design, there was nothing to slow the 20-gallon gush of water. So, instead of sending the tub's water flowing steadily down the drain, it flooded my bathroom.

Panicked at non-hurricane-related flooding, I raced into the kitchen to grab the mop. At the sight of his frantic, naked, human mother grabbing a mop, Meatloaf looked alarmed.

As I raced back toward my bathroom, I called back to Meatloaf, "Don't worry buddy, naked sprinting is my newest hobby!"

In the end, I sopped the water from the bathroom floor with bath towels. While normally this would be a suitable solution, without electricity these drenched towels could not be washed and dried afterwards. So, for the moment, I pushed them off, into a corner in the bathroom.

Wanting nothing more at that moment than a long, hot shower, I turned on the shower, waited for a few moments in the candlelight, then stepped into the flow of water.

*Holy mother of Sean! Frickin'. Cold. Shower.*

*Like a bull rider trying to hold on as long as possible, I frantically soaped and rinsed then jumped out after about 8 seconds. Dodging the end of the settee I grabbed for a towel but all the towels were dripping in a pile in the corner of the room. As the best alternative available, I grabbed a handful of washcloths from a nearby shelf and dried myself—very little bits at a time.*

# Comedians, Cats, and Cowboy's Beef

## Chapter 23

After writing in my journal, I needed to get out of the house. Pulling out of my garage, I re-entered a world that was still gray with the misted rain. As I drove through our town, it looked familiar but battered. Limbs, large and small, littered the streets. Many had already been moved to the streets' edges and blanketed the bike lanes. Still, others encroached into the lanes for driving, prompting cars to move with caution. Stoplights were still and black. At one intersection, a police officer motioned his hands, directing traffic around an uprooted but otherwise healthy tree that, plucked from the ground by Irma, had been left unceremoniously across three of four of the street's lanes.

Most places I passed were dark and closed. When I drew near a Starbucks with lights on, I stopped. Obviously powered by their own generators, Starbucks' hipster employees bustled back and forth, grinding beans, steaming milk, blending smoothies. Perhaps due to the contrast with the quiet that lay solidly across the rest of the town, this coffee shop seemed much louder than usual and the music grated on my nerves. Impatiently I waited for my latte but took it out to my car to drink it.

Since there was no way to know what restaurants and other businesses had power generators and which did not, I called around until I found one re-opened for business. So, I texted Nolan, Sean, and Peter to meet me at Hank's BBQ.

Peter's text message: "Hank's BBQ? Yee Haw!"

Sean: "Let's get sushi instead."

Me: "Every place with sushi is closed. It's either Hank's or Starbucks and in my opinion a Frappuccino does not a meal make."

Nolan: "Then put on your cowboy boots, boys! We're getting Southern BBQ!"

After our waiter sat pitcher-sized glasses of water on the table in front of each of us, Sean said, "Peter and I were talking, and we've come up with a new plan for you."

"Aren't we still in the middle of the last plan?" asked Nolan.

"Well yes, sweetie. This plan is in addition to the first plan. This is The Lemonade Plan," said Peter.

Nolan and I exchanged worried looks.

"No need to fret. You know how when life gives you lemons, you are supposed to make lemonade?" explained Peter.

Picking up from there, Sean said, "Well, what Peter means is that we've thought of a plan for you so you can turn this big pile of lemons into lemonade, you know, something good."

"The big pile of stuff David dropped on me doesn't smell like lemons to me," I said.

"It smells a lot like shi…" began Nolan

"Have ya'll decided what you'd like to order?" said our overly cheerful waiter, appearing suddenly at our table's side.

"Like I was saying, it seems more like we should figure out what we want to eat," said Nolan, trying to recover her conversational fumble.

"Why yes, young man', we absolutely should order," said Peter to the youthful waiter. Will you give us just one sec' to figure out what we've got a hankerin' for?"

"Yes, sir" he bobbed, smiling.

Soon Peter motioned the waiter back to our table then insisted the rest of us order first. When the turn to order came back to Peter, he said, "Yes sir, I think I will have your Cowboy's Beef!"

Sean stifled a laugh.

"The Cowboy Beef Brisket?" confirmed the waiter.

"Mmm hmm," confirmed Peter.

After the waiter left our table, Nolan said to Peter, "I think you just sexually harassed the waiter."

"Nope. If I sexually harassed the waiter, you wouldn't 'think', you'd know," said Peter with a wink.

"So, Peter, tell her the Lemonade Plan," said Sean.

"Ok, honey, here's the Lemonade Plan. It's very simple. There are only three steps: We think you should turn this David saga into a bestselling book

Then you should do a promotional tour in the town where David lives

Oh, and in preparation, you should up your training sessions with Hot Todd to 5 times a week to get you TV-ready."

"Um, Peter, was that a plan or was it just your subtle way of telling me I need to lose weight?"

Sean answered for him, "Oh no. You're not fat, Sloane. I think what Peter is saying is you are real-life thin but not TV thin."

"And that's supposed to make her feel better?" asked Nolan.

"Honey, all I'm saying is when you go on TV you want to look so hot that even the gays are like, "Da-mn, girl!""

"Well, gay is the highest standard," I said with a shrug. "But even so, I think you two have lost your minds. I'm an ACADEMIC. I only write things people read if they are assigned to read them as homework."

"Well, just think about it, Sloane. It would be so therapeutic," explained Sean.

"Seriously, you two are insane." Then, with a dismissive wave, I added, "Besides I don't need a new plan. I'm going back to my earlier man-plan," I said.

"Which is….?" Prompted Nolan.

"Remember before David and I got back together? My man-plan was to make either Jon Stewart, Stephen Colbert, or John Oliver my second husband, depending on whose wife died first."

"Oh Sloane, you're such a romantic," said Sean in a deadpan voice.

"Hey, I'm not actively hoping for one of their wives to die. I'm just saying that in the natural course of events, if one of those lovely ladies happens to bite it then I'm going to be the first one on the new widower's doorstep with a casserole," I said.

"For shame, Sloane!" said Peter, fanning himself with his napkin. "Again, I say, for shame Sloane!"

"Really! I'm not wishing them dead!" I said.

"No, that's not why Peter's shaming you," said Sean.

"I mean mirror, mirror on the wall; who is the hottest comedic genius of them all?" riddled Peter.

"Oh, you're talking about Trevor Noah, aren't you?" suggest Nolan.

"Um, yes! He is crazy yummy! Every time I watch the Daily Show, I just want to lick him like a Creamsicle." said Peter.

"Why isn't Trevor Noah on your list of possible second husbands?" asked Sean.

"Him? Well, I admit I'd love to put my pinky right in his sexy-cute dimple," I said.

"You look at a hottie, funny-man like Trevor Noah and all you think of is putting a pinky in his dimple? Are you kidding me?" mocked Sean.

"I can't put him on my second husband list because we have the same last name," I said. Seeing blank faces, I explained, "I have one colleague who took her husband's last name when they married. Now people still call her husband 'doctor' but most people just refer to her as 'Mrs.' now."

"Yeah, Sloane didn't go to school for 11 years after high school to be called 'Mrs. Noah' for the rest of her life," said Nolan.

Sean waived his hand dismissively, "Trevor is totally downside-worthy."

Peter stared at me intently, then with a raised eyebrow, "Oh, come on, Sloane! You know if Trevor let you put your pinky in his dimple, you'd want to Creamsicle the hell out of him!"

"I don't even know how I'd pinky-dimple him," I said.

"Trevor's smart. I bet he'd dig a brainy chick like you. You could promote one of your books on his show," suggested Sean.

"I write books about designing buildings," I said skeptically.

"She's right," said Peter, patting my hand. "Retirement housing design books are not going to get Sloane laid. That, my friends, is the genius of The Lemonade Plan!"

"Okay, then…" I said quickly to change the subject, "I read an interesting article about cats the other day."

Sean looked askew at Peter then said under his breath but loud enough for everyone at the table to hear, "Is she kidding?"

"Really. Did you know cats are obligate carnivores?"

"Oh God, she's not kidding," said Peter, eyes wide.

"What are obligate carnivores?" prompted Nolan.

"Apparently there are amino acids in meat that cats cannot make on their own. Unlike humans and a lot of other mammals, cats must eat other animals just to keep themselves alive," I explained.

"Oh, so they have to have blood like some kind of cute, little vampires?" asked Nolan.

"Nolan, stop encouraging the professor," said Peter with mock sternness.

Frowning at Peter, I continued, "Well strictly speaking, I'm unsure if the amino acids come from the blood or some other part; I'm not the right kind of doctor to be able to tell you that. Even so, the article made me think of David," I said.

"Flesh-eating felines made you think of your former fiancé?" asked Sean.

"Not the flesh-eating part but just the cats themselves," I said.

"Guide us through, sweetie. Guide us through," said Sean. "Everybody's lost."

Unable to resist the urge to explain the connection, I said, "Sean, you have a cat. Have you ever watched Jerry Potter stalk something?"

"Sure, Jerry loves to stalk squirrels," said Sean.

"When he stalks, does Jerry Potter arch his back, with all his hair standing on end or bear his claws?"

"No, of course not," said Sean.

"What does he do instead?" I asked.

"He smunches down," said Sean, crouching his shoulders in imitation, "then slowly and quietly sneaks up on the unsuspecting squirrel," said Sean.

"And then?" I prompted further.

"Then he stops to watch the squirrelly character until 'Womp!' He pounces!" explained Sean.

"Right. When does he arch his back and bear his claws?"

"When Mr. Potter's scared, he does that," answered Sean.

"Exactly," I said, looking around expectantly. Seeing only blank faces, I continued, "The squirrel isn't in danger when Jerry looks threatening. Instead of the danger being in the visible, it's hidden in the invisible."

"Okay, so, I think I'm with you," said Sean slowly. "Do you mean since David seemed like the consummate nice guy, that is what made him a threat?"

"Yes, exactly!" I said. "In other words, since he's so easy-going and gentle, it lulled me into a false sense of security. He didn't seem like a threat at all so I let down all my defenses."

"I see," said Nolan. "Then, with your defenses down, it was easier for him to trick you."

"Right," I said.

"Does that make you the mouse in this scenario? Oh God, and were you the mouse he played with before going in for the kill?" asked Peter.

"Well, sort of. That's the other interesting thing about cats—the way people think they play with their food."

"Huh?" said Sean.

"Well, cats don't play with their food to be cruel, even though cats may seem like fluffy, little sadists. What they are really doing when they play with a mouse before killing it is wearing out their prey. It is a strategy cats use to protect themselves from getting hurt," I explained.

"I see!" said Peter with sudden enthusiasm. The other two stared at Peter. Then Peter clarified, "It is because the cat is actually afraid of the mouse."

"That's right! The cat needs to minimize his risk in the situation because he is afraid. So, the cat plays with the mouse to make him less scary," I finished.

"So, Sloane's saying the cat's not cruel, he's just a big pussy!" exclaimed Peter.

"Wow, that is interesting," said Sean, nodding his head.

"I guess you were right, Sloane. David really is just a big vag'!" said Nolan.

Already in my stride, I continued, "For both David and the cat, what it all boils down to is cowardice. All the ridiculous lies and play-acting were because, more than anything, David was afraid I would reject him," I said.

"I hope that doesn't mean you feel sorry for him," said Nolan.

"No, I'm just saying it makes a little more sense to me now. It was so confusing before because I've known David long enough to know he isn't by nature cruel and yet he did something so awful," I said.

"Sloane, I'm really happy you understand it better—I know how important that is for you. Still," Sean said, now taking my hands in his, "please tell me even though you know he's intimidated by you, that you will still go ahead and crush him like a bug."

"No," said Nolan, looking at me appraisingly. "Sloane doesn't need to crush anyone. What Sloane needs is to be with someone who is as strong as she is."

"I just can't respect cowards. Maybe that's why I hate cats," I said.

Sean looked offended.

"Except for Jerry Potter, of course," I added.

"Does this mean you don't feel sad anymore?" asked Peter.

"No, I'm still sad. I'm just also realizing it would have been even worse for me if I married David *then* found out he was a coward," I said. "Nolan, what are my two big things?"

Ignoring Peter and Sean who glanced at my chest then one another, Nolan said, "Integrity and compassion. Those are Sloane's two must-haves when it comes to a partner."

"Right. And cowards can never truly have integrity because sometimes telling the truth is really hard. Telling difficult truths takes guts. A coward will lie whenever they feel uncomfortable," I said.

"It's a shame you wasted seven years of your life with that lying wuss, though," said Sean.

"I don't see it that way," I said. "I hate what he did—all the lies and deception—and I despise that he hurt my kids and so many people, but as long as I grow from this, I haven't lost anything. Instead I've only gotten stronger and better."

"Absolutely. And once you've grown and regained your balance, the time will come when you will meet someone who does have integrity and compassion," said Nolan.

"Seriously, thanks for that," I said with a sigh. "Just keep reminding me there is someone out there who is a better fit."

Sean looked thoughtful and asked, "After a break up, why is it that it always feels like you will never be in love again?"

"It's just an unfortunate side effect of break ups—the complete devaluation of self. But the self-loathing doesn't last forever. Then once you find your worth again, you realize it's the person who broke up with you who's the worthless sack," said Peter.

"Peter's right. Regardless of whatever value there is in David, he is not your equal, Sloane," said Sean.

"That's the nicest thing…" I said, going red.

Seeing the waiter coming with a tray, Peter interrupted, "Oh look, here comes my Cowboy's Beef! Yummy!"

# Secret Shopper

## Chapter 24

On Friday back at work, I tried to get myself into some kind of productive momentum. Working at a pace only slightly better than what could be labeled as wasting time, I was relieved to see a text from Sean on my phone.

Text from Sean: "Lunch?"

My text: "Twins need cough medicine. Drugstore lunch?"

Sean responded, "Your people really are barbarians."

"My people? Meaning single parents?"

"No!" said Sean, "I'm talking about breeders but yes to drugstore lunch (you know how I love to learn about other cultures)."

At noon, Sean walked into the store in his navy-blue scrubs. Seeing me waiting with a shopping basket slung over my forearm, Sean said with contrived seriousness, "Good day, doctor," then picked up an empty shopping basket for himself.

Since Sean was one of those people who was very natural at generating conversation, he was always an easy person to be around, even one-on-one. Soon though, he asked where I was on the whole starting to date again thing.

"I don't know. I'm broken. It doesn't seem right to hand only pieces of myself to someone."

"I still think you need to dip your toe in to test the waters, you know? I know a cute, straight guy at work. I could set you up; just for lunch or something easy."

"Eating lunch doesn't sound awful but eating lunch on a date does. Did Peter send you in today to talk me into going on a blind date?" I asked, suspiciously.

"Never," he claimed with false innocence.

Nearing the cold medicine isle, Sean said, "I've got to get stuff too. I'll meet you at checkout."

Without waiting for a response, Sean disappeared down a nearby aisle.

At the checkout counter, my basket held the needed cough medicine, a small bag of cashews, a box of chocolate Godiva cake truffles, and a can of the brand of over-priced bubbly water Sean and Peter had gotten Nolan and I hooked on about a year ago. Waiting in line behind a woman with steeply curved shoulders and tightly curled gray hair, I watched as she carefully took an item from her basket, sat it on the counter gently, then straightened the item as though perfect alignment was necessary before the product could be tossed into a plastic bag. Slowly again, she pulled a second item from her basket and repeated the routine.

Enthralled with her meticulous process, I did not see Sean until he tapped me on the shoulder from behind. As I turned toward him, he launched into an enthusiastic telling of a story about the drugstore having Cupcake brand Cabernet and Sauvignon Blanc but not having Cupcake Pinot Noir, except during the holidays, apparently. Distracted by his zeal, I was surprised as he dumped the contents of his basket into mine then, pushed a $50.00 bill into my hand as he said, "I'm buying," then rushed off to put away his basket.

Having turned away from the meticulous shopper lady to talk to Sean, now I realized the person behind me in line was my boss from the University.

"Dr. Noah," my boss said with a reserved nod.

"Dr. Newport," I answered.

"Doing well I hope?" asked Dr. Newport.

The meticulous shopper took her bags gingerly from the cashier then shuffled off. While answering I hurried to unload my basket, "Yes, thanks. Busy as always. Trying to get that grant application together with that new assistant professor in Occupational Therapy."

As I finished the thought, I noticed the expression on Dr. Newport's face change from moderate interest to surprise. Following his gaze, I looked at my items while still moving them from basket to counter. Startled too, I saw a box of Trojan's Ultra-Sensitive condoms in my hand which I sat beside a bottle of Cupcake Cabernet, a tube of lubricant, a brown bottle of Hershey's Chocolate Syrup, and a pair of plastic handcuffs. *I'm going to kill Sean,* I thought.

"Gag gift," I said to Dr. Newport with a shrug then turned around before my face burst into flames.

As Sean and I walked into the CVS parking lot, I growled, "What the hell?!"

Sean blinked innocently at me.

"Seriously, my boss was in line behind me!" I continued.

Stifling a laugh, Sean waved his hand dismissively and said, "People have sex. And bosses are people."

"Oh no! No!" I corrected, "Most bosses are people but, in this case, there is a statistically significant likelihood that Newport is a robot!"

Sean grinned, "Maybe robots have sex too?"

"And why do I need chocolate sauce and handcuffs to have intercourse?" I huffed just above a whisper.

"Well, if you don't know that then you really *do* need to get out more," said Sean. "And call it 'sex', Sloane. Nobody's going to want to bang you if you keep calling it intercourse."

"I can't say 'sex' in a drugstore," I said, whispering my retort.

"You're being weird," said Sean.

"And with whom am I supposed to be having this sticky-chocolate, handcuff *sex* with anyway?" I pressed.

"Peter and I just wanted to give you a little get-back-on-the-stud-horse gift basket of sorts. Think of it as a gentle nudge back into the dating world."

"I am still miles away from Cupcake Cabernet and lubrication."

"We're just trying to be optimistic, sweetie," said Sean, patting me affectionately on the head. "Plus, fingers crossed for a dead comedian's wife in the near future!"

"Well, next time keep your optimism in your own shopping basket!" I snapped.

# Damsel or Hero

## Chapter 25

"Nolan, I need to write back to Melissa, David's wife. I'm sure she's anxious for a response," I said from the other end of the phone call.

"Well, no matter how you look at it, that will not be an easy message to write," responded Nolan.

"Should I even give her advice? Even though she asked for it, it seems, well, kind of twisted that the advice will be coming from me. I am, after all, her husband's mistress."

"Yes, it's twisted but since this whole situation is twisted, it makes sense in context," said Nolan. "Plus, the poor woman must not have her own tribe of friends since she came to you asking for help."

"Poor woman. Imagine going through this mess without the love and support of your tribe, who also on occasion put chocolate syrup and handcuffs into your shopping basket."

"Seriously, if she's alone in her pain, she needs someone to help her through it; she may not be able to rescue herself," said Nolan.

"So, in this situation, is she the damsel in distress?"

"Yes, so that means you need to be the hero."

"Well, I don't know that I'm properly equipped for heroics. For God's sake, I can't even walk in heels!" I said.

"Didn't you tell me the other day that the characteristics all heroes have are integrity and bravery?"

"It's really annoying when you paraphrase me back to me."

"Take it as a complement. Apparently, everyone takes turns being the damsel in distress and at other times everyone gets the opportunity to be a hero," explained Nolan. "The key, I think, is that being a damsel in distress just happens, but being a hero has to be a conscious choice."

I stayed quiet.

"I think Melissa needs you to step in and be her temporary tribe; she needs you to lend her some of your strength," suggested Nolan.

"I can do that; I'm citrus, remember?"

"Ah yes, your strength is in being small, flexible, and able to bend in the direction the wind is blowing," said Nolan.

"What if I say the wrong thing, though, then it all gets worse for her?" I asked.

"You won't. You're just going to show her how to grow when you get a bunch of shit dumped on you."

"I am getting quite practiced at that."

"Yes, growth is the upside of crap!" said Nolan.

"And if I do say all the wrong things, I will just send her a basket of oranges."

"Now that I think about it, you're really lucky to be on this side of it. If you married David this past summer like you'd planned, this could be you—the damsel with the cheating husband."

"Wow, "I said then after a pause, "You are absolutely right. Really, that was a close call, a very close call. Thank goodness David fake-died when he did." I paused again. "I can't believe I'm going to say this but I am so glad this worked out the way it did."


Friday, 11:01 P.M.

Dear Melissa,

Since I don't really know you and considering my role in this, I couldn't possibly advise you on what you should do. But you didn't ask what you should do but rather asked what I would do if I found myself in your position. So here it goes…

Are there some really great things about David? Sure.

Do I still love him? Yes. Even now.

Is he who I imagined growing old with? Yes.

Even so, and I can't state this firmly enough, I would *never, ever* give that man the opportunity to hurt me again. In my opinion some things are unforgivable, and what he has done is miles past that line.

If I stayed with him, I would never be at ease because he cannot be trusted. Every time he put his hands on me, I'd cringe wondering who else he'd been touching.

I wouldn't be able to look myself in the face for staying with someone who has shown me so little respect. And worse yet, I couldn't justify to myself knowing I was putting him in a position in which he could do it again. For me, now, he's part of my past but I'll be damned before I let him have any part in my future.

Do keep in mind, though, that is me and you must find the path that is best-suited for you.

Sincerely,

Sloane

# Chocolate-Coated Disaster

## Chapter 26

Go Team 2
Doctor Deceived

By Sloane Noah

The flashing from Dr. Design's Fitbit woke her from a sound sleep.

"…This is a Go Team 2 Alert…On the shoulder of I-75 Southbound, Douche-monks are suspected in overturning a semi-trailer truck carrying Godiva Chocolate's new secret recipe cake truffle flights. Said delectable cargo has spilled out across the interstate. In this atrocity, the truck driver, Mary McCotter, was taken hostage. Mission: Mary McCotter and the Truffles of Secret will commence on the scene immediately. This message will automatically delete in 3…2…1…"

Before her Fitbit blinked white, Dr. Design was already dressed in her standard-issue Go Team 2 uniform—the black unitard with her identifying emblem—an artistic rendition of an LED light bulb crossed by a drafting pencil and architect's scale. While our unsuspecting hero dashed off into the night, little did she know that the other Go Team 2 members still slept soundly because Dr. Design's sham alert was the first part of a diabolical ruse.

With innumerable concerned interstate drivers stopped and parked along the roadside, the scene was pandemonium. Among the chaos, brave individuals risked their own safety to rescue any of the thousands of victims of this attack—the secret-recipe chocolate cake truffles. With good Samaritans swarming the scene, cars still traveling down the interstate were being forced off the road to avoid hitting these brave folks or worse, the chocolate confections!

Shouts and squealing tires were mixed with the sound of the rising wind. Dr. Design scanned the scene carefully. With her superhuman eye for detail, Dr. Design searched for the other Go Team 2 members but they were nowhere in sight. Dr. Design's mind considered the variables and used her re-built Smith Corona Mega Processor 5000 to quickly perform a multi-attribute utility theory statistical analysis to mathematically prioritize the possible options in the situation. Based on the analysis, the results indicated she had no choice but to search alone for the douche-monk suspects and kidnapped driver until the other Go Team 2 members arrived. That's when she spotted some unusual activity off in the distance, near some old railroad tracks.

As Dr. Design moved stealthily toward the tracks, she could see a woman—presumably Mary McCotter the truck driver—gagged and tied to the tracks in classic damsel-put-in-distress-via-retro-style-villainy. Dr. Design's keen mind knew instantly an on-coming train was not a danger as these tracks were being considered for conversion into biking trails. *What was this douche-monk criminal thinking?* Dr. Design thought to herself as she vaulted over a nearby fence, hurdled several shrubs then was at Ms. McCotter's side.

Just as Dr. Design removed the gag from the driver's mouth, two things happened simultaneously. Dr. Design felt strong hands grip her shoulders from behind and Mary McCotter screamed, "Look out!" But it was too late! Dr. Design was already in the douche-monk's clutches. Even worse, this was no ordinary douche-monk. This was The Douche-Monk Supreme!

On this humid, windy night, The Douche-Monk Supreme pulled Dr. Design away from the tracks. Spouting a prolonged string of well-practiced, alluring words as they moved past a swamp and towards a remote orange grove. Fearing this day might come, Dr. Design tried to block out The Douche-Monk Supreme's sugary sentiments. Still, the honeyed yet painful sentences gushed on and on from his mouth, like water from a firehose.

At last, these persuasive romanticisms started lulling Emotion—one of the weakest characters in Dr. Design's finely-honed mind—into a hypnotic state. A moment before it was too late, Dr. Design sent out a partial distress signal to the other Go Team 2 members via her Fitbit which read "Near truffle accident held by…" Then resistance was futile.

Receiving the incomplete distress message, the remaining Go Team 2 members struck out to rescue Dr. Design but would they be able to find and rescue her in time?

Meanwhile, Dr. Design found herself captive under the largest tree in the orange grove. The Douche-Monk Supreme continued his barrage of compliments, apologies, explanations, and assurances.

Before long, the soliloquy incorporated invitations and proposals of plans and a future. Then in coordination with his verbal bombardment, The Douche-Monk Supreme advanced with his final assault. In this, he handed Dr. Design a pen and a marriage license on which everything had been filled in save Dr. Design's signature. In Dr. Design's spellbound state, she felt giddy and euphoric.

The other Go Team 2 members were now on the scene next to the overturned semi. That's when they heard a woman's voice shouting from a distance. The General listened with her bat-like hearing and led the group toward the call for help.

Soon the Go 2s found the panicked Mary McCotter ungagged but still bound to the tracks. While untying the many Boy Scout-perfect clove hitch knots holding her, Mary relayed as much of the tale as she could.

"And that's when the man pulled the woman in black away in that direction," Mary explained, pointing.

With the woman now unbound, the Go Team 2 members formed a single line and advanced methodically through the windy darkness in the direction indicated.

Vaguely as though from under water or perhaps from a great, great distance, Dr. Design could hear people calling for someone. *Who were they looking for?* She wondered dimly. Feeling warm and secure, wrapped snugly in The Douche-Monk Supreme's appeal, Dr. Design did not even notice the intensifying wind that grasped at the paper and pen foisted into her hands.

After the wind ebbed briefly, an ardent burst made the trees tremble, punctuating the air with the sounds of shuddering of leaves and quaking branches. As the surge swept through the canopy of the large tree above, a small branch with two leaves and a single orange broke free, dropped, and ricocheted off the top of Dr. Design's pony-tailed head before falling to the ground with a small *thud*.

Whether it was the blow on the head from the sweetly-scented orb or the small thump sound, Dr. Design could not say. But something loosened a piece of memory in her mind. Even with her mental faculties still confined by the emotional hijacking, the barf chunk of memory broke free inside Dr. Design's mind. With that tiny bit of memory resurfacing, a small hole punched through the dam blocking her thinking. Then, as the regurgitated memory picked up momentum, the area around the hold began crumbling. Soon, this gave-way to an even larger opening permitting Dr. Design to once again access her mind.

Suddenly, Intellect and his buddy Logic came flooding back into Dr. Design's head, like a 20-gallon tub of cold water tipped over in a Mid-Century Modern style shower. Doused alert by these insights, Dr. Design came to her senses.

Thrusting the pen and unsigned paper back into The Douche-Monk Supreme's hands, Dr. Design said, "No thanks. Your crap already helped me grow so I don't need any more of it."

"What the...?" started The Douche-Monk Supreme. Just then, Mastercraft and The General grabbed him while Cutter started binding him with what looked like a roll of surgical tape.

Just as the earliest morning light peeked into the grove, Dr. Design picked up the fallen orange from the ground and said, to no one in particular, "I'm going to keep this though. The fruit is the best part." Then, leaving the bound man behind in the grove, Go Team 2 walked off together to live lightly, then heavily and back and forth like that ever after, you see?

# Ashes to Ashes

## Chapter 27

After the twins came home from their dad's house the next day, we exchanged stories about our time apart during Hurricane Irma's visit to town. Once each tale was told and every stomach was sufficiently stuffed with snacks, I gathered all of my strength to tell them the recently discovered truth about David.

"I do need to tell you two something important. Recently, I got some very shocking news about David which was upsetting to me and may be upsetting to you," I began.

The twins just stared at me, wide-eyed.

"What I found out is David didn't actually die from cancer as we were told. Apparently, he was living a whole other life we didn't know anything about. By that, I mean he is actually alive and living with the woman he used to be divorced from in addition to his kids."

Beck was the first to break the silence that followed, "What the hell?!" he yelled.

"I know, it's shocking. It was all very hard for me to believe at first. Since I needed to know the truth of the situation, I even hired a private investigator to find out what was actually going on."

Shaking her head slowly in disbelief, Avery said, "I, I, I just don't know what to say." With tears starting to roll down her cheeks, "It seems like that just can't be possible."

"Why would? How could? Why?" stammered Beck.

"I don't really know why. I do know we did not do anything wrong that led to this."

"I wish he *was* dead!" roared Beck as he marched from the room, leaving the house through the front door.

After the door banged shut, still tearful, Avery said, "Mom, I don't even know how to think about this."

"I know exactly what you mean," I said pulling her into a hug. Encircled in my arms, Avery's remaining reserve evaporated, then she wept. Slightly taller than I, Avery sobbed loudly into my shoulder.

Holding her even more tightly, I said with tears now streaking my face, "This is all very upsetting and we might feel sad for quite a while. And that's okay. We will be sad when we need to be and mad when we need to be. Eventually, we will feel better again."

Avery took a deep breath, then wailed louder.

"I love you, sweetheart. We are strong so I know we are going to get through this."

Just then, the front door crashed open and Beck reappeared. Already crying openly, he kicked the door closed with the back of his foot then he rushed to join in our blubbering hug.

"Mom," Beck said as though to confirm my presence.

"I love you so much," I said drawing Beck into the hug. "I was just telling Avery that even though this might make us sad and mad for some time, that is okay. We have every right to be upset. Then, after we feel all these hard feelings, we are going to be alright. This is not our faults."

There was silence except for Avery's loud sobs into my shoulder and Beck weeping onto the top of my head. I cried quietly, and held them as tight as I could.

As the days crawled forward, sometimes David seemed to be all we talked about. Other days, we did not mention him at all. At some point, the occasional day of not speaking about him stretched into multiple days. Even though that seemed like an improvement, the days we did talk about him became increasingly fueled by anger. Although I encouraged the twins to talk about their feelings openly, one evening I decided to try something different.

After work, I came home carrying an over-sized, plastic shopping bag. Attracted by the prospect of gifts, the twins gathered around me. Feeling like a jaded St. Nick, I pulled out two plastic Whiffle ball bats, handing one to each of them. Each twin accepted their yellow, lightweight bat but exchanged confused looks with one another. Next, I took two dark colored Fuggler Funny Ugly Monsters from the sack. The stuffed monster dolls were the same—charcoal-colored with tufts of black hair, a wide toothy grimace, and gray button eyes. Again, the twins accepted the age-inappropriate offering.

With the baffled twins frozen in place and staring at me expectantly, I presented an explanation, "I know we've all been feeling pretty pissed at David lately."

Beck snorted then rolled his eyes but I continued, "And of course we are pissed. We have every right to be. So, I thought it might help if you guys could get out some of your frustrations on these Ugly Monsters that have hair and eyes similar in color to David's."

Smiles spread across their faces then Avery stepped back and said, "It's all you, Beck!" as she tossed her Ugly Monster in a high arch towards Beck. Eying the incoming monster, Beck swung hard with his yellow bat and the Ugly Monster/pretend David flew across the room.

"My turn now!" squealed Avery. Then, Beck pitched his monster toward Avery.

"And Avery hits it out of the park," Beck commentated as the second Monster sailed across the room.

That was followed by laughter and more monster throwing. For a while, I stood and watched, feeling satisfied with my purchases. After a time, the twins' monster bashing got louder and rowdier. Clearly there was no need for me to officiate so I pulled a magazine off a nearby shelf then walked toward my room. Confused by the ruckus, Meatloaf followed closely behind me.

Not long after I finished reading the magazine, there was a knock on my bedroom door. Without waiting for a response, Avery threw the door open and said, "Mom, come quick!"

Alarmed, I rushed after Avery as she raced to the family room. There, stood Beck and beside him was Nolan.

"So, your kiddos called because they were concerned that you didn't have your own monster doll," Nolan explained. Before the sentence was complete, the twins began racing in and out of rooms and opening and closing cabinets and drawers.

Ignoring the commotion, Nolan continued but in a louder voice, "They suggested we buy you your own monster and bat, but I had another idea."

Like a gameshow model showcasing prizes, Avery gestured toward the kitchen island where a large pile of items now sat.

Beck picked up Nolan's thread, "So Auntie Nolan thought…"

"And we agree," piped Avery.

"That we should go back to the basics," finished Beck with a nod.

"Yes," said Nolan. "Sloane, do you remember what we used to do in college when we went through a bad break up?"

"Of course," I said. "We'd go to the nearest state park, pack one of those concrete BBQ grills full of stuff they left with us like T-shirts and pictures, then we'd have a Boyfriend BBQ."

"Precisely!" exclaimed Beck as he turned to help Avery stuff the items sitting on the counter into fabric shopping bags. Before carrying the bagged items out to the backyard, Avery paused long enough to hand me a lighter and starter fluid.

"Don't we need to go to the park?" I questioned Nolan as she shuffled me towards the back door.

Outside, Beck gestured towards the bags now sitting next to our metal backyard firepit and said, "Mom, you do the honors!"

"Okay," I said as I pulled one of David's T-shirts I used to sleep in from the bag, "but everyone needs to help!" Then I tossed the shirt into the firepit.

Soon, from an almost empty bag, Avery removed a ceramic platter painted with David and my initials intertwined, it was one I made at one of those pottery painting places we went to with David.

Since pottery is not a good source of kindling, we all paused for a moment. Then I said, "I know!" as I ran off, disappearing into the garage.

The twins and Nolan followed me onto the driveway. Moments later, I popped out of the open garage. First, I gave Avery a dustpan and Beck the garage broom, the one we only used to sweep our porches and the garage. Next, I handed everyone a pair of safety goggles then put a pair of them on myself.

"Everybody, stand back!" I called, holding out one arm dramatically.

Each of them took a couple steps toward the driveway's edges. Raising the platter over my head with both hands, "Be gone from our minds and hearts, David—you cruel douche-monkey!" I proclaimed, slamming the platter hard toward the waiting pavement.

Ceramic shards flew in all directions. Since several larger pieces remained, the twins gathered these then smashed them to the pavement a second time.

After asking the twins to sweep up the scattered pieces, Nolan and I headed toward the backyard again. Before we made it to the red, freestanding fire pit, the twins raced past us, with Avery carrying a cardboard box now containing all the platter's broken pieces.

At the fire pit, Avery offered Beck the box with exaggerated formality, "Brother, would you like to do the honors?"

"Thank you, sister, but I think you should let our dear mother do it," responded Beck in kind.

Accepting the box from Avery's hands, I held it stiffly in front of me.

With ceremonial formality, I preached, "Ashes to ashes, dust to dust; may our sorrow and hurt return to the ground from whence the dirtbag David Langer sprung."

After I poured the broken pieces onto the items already in the fire pit, Beck said, "I get to help light it!"

He squeezed starter fluid onto the pile. When I told him that was enough, Beck paused, looked up at me, eyes wide in feigned innocence, then squeezed the starter fluid bottle briefly once more.

"I'm sorry, mother, that was an unfortunate mishap," he said in his stuffiest tone.

"Well played, I said.

While telling everyone to step back, I pulled the last item remaining from the bags. It was a greeting card from David. Holding the card in my hand, I lit one corner with the lighter. As the flame sprung to life then rapidly grew, I tossed the burning card on top of the lighter fluid-doused pile. The pile crackled and popped to life.

Flames leapt and smoke rose for almost an hour. Once only glowing ashes remained, I asked Avery to bring me a shovel and a pair of work gloves. With Avery back in a flash, I put on the heavy, leather gloves then picked up the shovel. I started digging a hole in the ground beside the place where the metal firepit was perched. The twins exchanged glances but said nothing, sensing this was an important moment. Once the hole was deep enough, I used my thickly gloved hands to tilt the firepit, letting the debris fall into the hole.

Then I picked up the shovel again to cover the pile of ash and pottery shards with the mound of dirt I'd just created. When all the soil was returned to the now-filled hole, I tapped the fresh mound with the backside of my shovel, packing the earth down with a satisfying sense of finality.

Both twins looked at me expectantly.

Avery said, "What happens now?"

Nolan answered, "Well, in college we'd usually head to the bar afterwards."

Tossing the shovel aside, I said, "In this case, we'd probably be best served by going out for the biggest ice cream sundaes we can find."

"Yes!" shouted Beck, punching one arm into the air.

Accompanied by their whoops and yells, the twins raced back toward the house.

Pausing before going in, Avery turned and exclaimed, "You're my hero, mom!"

As Nolan and I turned to walk towards the house as well, Nolan wrapped an arm around my shoulder, giving it a squeeze, and with a grin said, "See, I told you that you were the hero in this story."

Returning her smile, I said nothing because, really, what more was there to *say*? My tribe had spoken.

Later, in the night's quiet, there was one message I needed to write before I could rest. I typed it first as a text message then copied the text to send in an email as well. These read:

> *David, your weakness and selfishness broke my heart. At the very least, I deserved an explanation from you, yet you hid, hoarding your reasons and excuses. While you skulked like an insect in the dark, I grew, like a wild flower rising from broken ground. Tomorrow's a new day, my day. And you will never trample me again.*

Afterwards I lay in bed, feeling freer than I had in a very long time. Almost giddy with fatigue, I felt as though I had just run a very long race. Still, I didn't have an explanation nor an apology but I no longer felt as though my life was stalled until I had those. It was likely I'd never truly know why David made the choices he did. Even though I still carried the heavy weight of my unanswered questions, I was strong enough to carry these and keep moving forward. While demons—long dismissed—can still rise-up from time-to-time, I knew I would face them when they did; I had strength enough to be my own hero now. That's because in my own hurricane, I bent but didn't break.

# Excrement, Unsolicited Advice & Growing Wild

## Afterword

Encountering assholes and their consequent shit is part of the human experience. When dumped upon—as invariably happens from time to time—I try to remember these things:

1) People are a lot like plants.
2) Poop is a long-valued fertilizer, which promotes plant growth.
3) Big dump = more fertilizer
4) It may stink to holy hell but that stench is actually the scent of potential growth & positive change.
5) For shit to become fertilizer, it needs to cure and that, as well as growth, takes time. So, sometimes, that means waiting and waiting until the new growth is ready to start.

Even the rarest, hardest to grow flowers will thrive with the right fertilizer. Plant-lovers have been proving this for eons in their greenhouses stocked with exotic plants. While I appreciate the challenge of growing delicate flowers appeals to some, difficult, rare flowers never interested me. Instead, I find wildflowers much more impressive than flowering plants that grow only in perfect nursery conditions. That's precisely because wildflowers do not require special care or conditions to thrive.

If fertilizer comes along by happenstance, wildflowers will use it. Similarly, come storm or stampede, wildflowers will work with whatever circumstances they encounter. Regardless of the obstacle, wildflowers simply accept what is, look for the light, and keep working to expand their simple, honest beauty.

www.ingramcontent.com/pod-product-compliance
Lightning Source LLC
Chambersburg PA
CBHW031027260626
47153CB00017B/2752